HIS PLEDGE TO HONOR

A SILVER STAR RANCH ROMANCE

SHANAE JOHNSON

THOSE JOHNSON GIRLS

Scout Silver walked the length of the solicitor's office. The office wasn't on the main street of the small Montana town she'd lived all her life in. The town was only considered small due to its population. The square footage of Honor Valley could fit the island of Manhattan inside a couple of times. But the people could all fit into the high school football stadium with enough elbow room to be comfortable. Though they'd all likely be hugging each other while mixing and mingling.

So, no, she didn't have to drive the thirty minutes it would take her to get into the heart of the town to handle her business. She'd only had to saddle up a horse and ride next door to her neighbor's at the Flying Cross Ranch.

Scout hadn't even bothered to knock at the front door of the Matthews's homestead. The massive door was always open. She'd walked right in and let herself into the converted formal living room, which served as Haran Matthews's office, to wait.

Instead of waiting in one of the six chairs pulled into the room, she paced.

The familiar surroundings should've eased her spirit. There was the ancient oak desk under which she'd never been found in games of hide and seek. The well-tread afghan of fading reds and blues whose patterns she'd focus on when she was being scolded for some childish indiscretion that had never been her idea, yet she'd taken the blame to protect the younger, guilty party.

It was the pictures on the wall that had always fascinated her most. She looked up at those now. Most of the pictures featured tall, uniformed Black men in black and white reproductions and sepia-toned prints. The black and white print was a snapshot of the 9th Cavalry Regiment known as the Buffalo Soldiers; the all-Black soldiers who fought in the American Civil War. The sepia-toned photograph was a picture of the Tuskegee Airman; another all-Black force of airman from the century just past. The third picture was in full color. It featured a skinny Black man with his arm around a barrel-chested white man. Both men sported the modern camouflage style of military fatigues, handle-bar mustaches, and broad, toothsome grins that told the viewer that they were solemnly up to no good.

Scout reached her hand up to the picture. With a tremble in her index finger, she traced the line of the white man's smile. She tried with all her might not to blink because whenever she did, the picture of her father faded in her mind.

The door of the office opened. Scout jerked her hand away from the photograph on the wall. Her features went carefully blank. Her eyes trained on the afghan as though expecting punishment for the indiscretion.

A white man with a handlebar mustache did not enter the room. Nor did a whiskered Black man. The door opened to reveal a head of dark brown hair much like her own. But Saylor's hair was pulled back in a tight ponytail rather than loose and down her shoulders like Scout's.

"We're the first two to arrive?" asked Saylor.

"Just like always." Scout opened her arms to her younger sister. The two eldest of the Silver sisters embraced in the empty room, holding onto each other like they were all they had because now that was true.

"I still don't understand why we're here?" said Saylor. "The General's funeral was three months ago."

Scout shrugged helplessly. "I didn't even know he'd left a will. The only thing he owned was the ranch, which he signed over to mom after the first time they got divorced."

"No, that was actually the second time they got divorced," Saylor corrected.

Saylor scratched at her nose. When she did so, Scout noticed the bags under her sister's eyes. Either Saylor wasn't sleeping well, or she had been crying last night. Scout wouldn't be surprised if both were true. Though she doubted the tears had anything to do with their father's death three months ago.

General Abraham Silver's daughters had been prepared for this day since their birth. Their father, who'd enlisted right out of high school, had been one of the original Navy SEALS. By the time Scout was born, he'd been leading elite covert operations for a decade. His life was in danger more times than it was not.

"Father Matthews didn't tell you anything?" asked Saylor.

Scout shook her head, her gaze returning to the picture on the wall. She eyed the sly smile of the man with his arm around her father. Just like the biblical brothers in the Bible, Haran Matthews and Abraham Silver had been like true brothers. So much so that Abe's daughters had always called their father's best friend and neighbor Father. It was a happy coincidence that the veteran and lawyer was also a man of the cloth.

"If there is a will," said Saylor, "do you think Cruella will contest it?"

Scout cringed at the mention of their father's second wife. That divorce had been a battlefield with many casualties, namely the children. Their stepmother Catherine had tried to take the ranch in the settlement, which had been the main reason why their father had signed the Silver Star Ranch over to their mother the second time they'd remarried.

"I don't know," said Scout. "But I have a bad feeling about this."

"Cruella didn't even show up to the funeral. But I know Mareen's here."

As though she heard her name being called, the product of that second marriage walked into the door. Mareen's elegance preceded her as she framed the doorway.

As always, her head was high. The makeup coating her porcelain skin was perfectly done to accentuate the crystal blue eyes they all shared. Instead of cowboy boots like Scout wore, or penny loafers like Saylor wore, Mareen wore six-inch stilettos, which were entirely impractical on a ranch. She had for a short time, but then she'd chosen sides. And that side had been away from the ranch with her high society mother.

"Ladies," Mareen said.

Ladies. Not sisters. Not family.

Though Saylor and Mareen could've been twins with how much they favored. Instead of a ponytail, Mareen's hair was coiffed in a perfect bun. Scout knew the woman's eyesight was as poor as her sisters, but Mareen wore contacts.

Irish twins was a term Scout had heard whispered behind the hands of the town gossips. Ghetto twins was what she'd heard thrown at Saylor's back in the halls of school. Both Saylor and Mareen were technically the second eldest of the Silver sisters. Both women were twenty-five. Born the same year. But to different mothers.

Scout and Saylor shared a look. Scout motioned

her head for Saylor to say something. Saylor raised her brows and shook her head. Scout rolled her eyes.

Mareen turned to glance at them. Just in time for Scout and Saylor to straighten and smile blandly. Suspicion cut the corners of Mareen's blue eyes, but like always, she said nothing, offering her older sisters the silent treatment.

The three eldest Silver sisters were saved by a clamor coming through the door. It was the youngest three Silver sisters. The identical faces of Tilly and Gunny came through the door first. Their blonde hair a hallmark from their mother -their father's third wife.

Well, technically Roxanne had been their father's fourth marriage. After the General left Mareen's mom, he'd come back home. For a short time. But her parent's second marriage lasted the blink of an eye.

The timeline was all too confusing when Scout was busy learning Algebra, so she'd stopped trying to work out the equation and all its variables. She was simply thrilled to have two new products of the complex math; Gunnery and Artillery.

Yes, the names were tragic. All their names were tragic. It just proved how head over heels each of her father's three wives must have been for him to allow that ink to dry on the birth certificates.

Scout had vowed at a young age that she would never be that head over heels for a boy. She'd had a couple of boyfriends over the years. But each relationship had confirmed her commitment to never get married and save herself the drama that the institution caused.

Surprisingly, her sisters didn't share the same view. Saylor was head over heels with a man who Scout knew was a one-way ticket to a divorce attorney. Luckily, Scout doubted the philanderer would ever take her sister down the aisle. Then there was Mareen, who sported a blinding rock on her left hand.

"I'll bet dad left us all a secret stash of money," said Brig, the youngest and last of the six Silver sisters. "You know he didn't trust banks. He probably left piles with Father Matthews, and that's why he's called us here today."

Brigadear Silver looked exactly like Scout and Saylor with her dark hair and light eyes. Because, like Scout and Saylor, Brig shared the same mother and father. After his third wife, which was his fourth marriage, Abraham Silver came back to his first wife once more. Apparently, the third time was a charm because they stayed married until her mom died ten years ago.

But once Sarah Silver was laid to rest, the girls rarely saw their father again. He dove into his work with the military, rarely surfacing for more than the occasional phone call with his girls.

"Hey Mareen, you came back," said Brig, her bright eyes glowed as she flung herself at Mareen.

"Of course, I did." Mareen offered her youngest sibling an awkward pat on the back and a tight smile. There was some give to Mareen's smile.

Brig was a force of nature. She was also too young to have felt the carnage of all the adults' emotional warfare. But honestly, Scout simply doubted the young woman cared.

Brig took the seat next to Mareen and began chatting away about her studies at the state school she was attending. Mareen tried to hold her aloof composure. But it was slipping under Brig's easygoing, tornado-like friendliness.

The door opened for the fourth time. Part of Scout worried that they might be introduced to a seventh sibling. But no, it wasn't another pale-skinned woman with brown hair and blue eyes that entered. It was a dark-skinned man with a handlebar mustache. The grin that had always hinted at mischief was thin right now.

Scout had always viewed Haran Matthews as the strongest man she knew, stronger even than her father because he had come back home to raise and care for his family. Father Matthews was from a line of warriors. His great grandfather was one of the Buffalo Soldiers depicted on the wall. His own father had been one of the Tuskegee Airmen.

But Father Matthews looked small and tired today. Scout had to remind herself that he had lost his best friend. The weight of the loss, and whatever their father had tasked him to do in his absence, was clearly heavy on his shoulders.

He looked around the room, not quite meeting any of the girls' eyes. That's when the bad feeling in Scout's stomach increased. There was one seat left open, but she wanted to pace the floor. She wanted to crawl under the massive oak desk and hide. Instead, she trained her gaze to the floor and counted the patterns on the rug. Whatever Father Matthews was about to tell them, she knew she would be in trouble.

Father Matthews rounded the desk. He looked pointedly at Scout. Finally, she took the seat. Once she was seated, he sat too.

"Girls, I have your father's last will and testament here." Father Matthews took a deep breath before continuing. "He's left you all equal shares of the ranch."

"But I thought Mom left the ranch to Scout?" said Tilly.

Tilly and Gunny's mother had died shortly after their birth. When their father had shown up on his ex-wife's doorstep with two infants in tow, Sarah Silver hadn't blinked an eyelash. She'd taken the bundles in and raised them as her own.

"When your parent's remarried the last time, the property became both of theirs," Father Matthews was saying. "When your mother died, it reverted back to your father."

Scout sat forward. She hadn't known that. All this time, she'd been carrying on running the day to day operation of the Silver Star Ranch as though she were the sole owner. She'd converted the homestead into a horse rehabilitation ranch and taken on injured, abandoned, and discarded horses and gave them a place where they could heal and recover. The business didn't make her rich, but it paid the bills, including the education of her sisters.

"Well, I'm giving my part to you, Scout," said

Gunny. "You've taken care of all of us since mom died."

"I agree," said Tilly.

In her peripheral vision, Scout saw Brig and Saylor both nod their agreement. Mareen's chin didn't dip. It remained high, and she stared straight ahead.

"I'm afraid it's not that simple," said Father Matthews. "You see, your father left stipulations. One of which being that the will couldn't be read until three months after his passing. The other stipulation..."

Father Matthews set down the stack of papers. He closed his eyes and pinched the hairs at the edge of his mustache.

Scout had seen her father make that same motion. He often did it when he was arguing with her mother. Or when he was disciplining one of his daughters. Again, Scout's gaze tracked down to the afghan, seeking the pattern while she awaited a punishment for an act that wasn't her doing.

"As I said, your father wrote that the land reverts to each of his daughters equally. However, before any of you can sell or transfer your portions..." Father Matthews took another gulp, still avoiding each of their gazes. "Before any of you can transfer your ownership, you'll have to get married."

There was silence in this room that had always been filled with so much laughter, a little scolding, and the deep baritone of Father Matthews telling stories of old to his children and the children of his best friend.

"Married?"

"Married!"

"Married."

Only Scout, Saylor, and Mareen remained mute at the proclamation.

Father Matthews held up his hand as though he weren't done. But what more could there be?

"If you're not all married within the year of your father's passing, the land goes..." And now Father Matthews did look up. He looked up to Scout. "...to his second wife, Catherine."

CHAPTER TWO

*L*incoln Rawlings rolled his head around his neck. The popping sounds of the tendons there set his nerves on high alert. Gunfire had been a constant siren call in his living quarters for years, never allowing him to fully relax where he lay his head.

For a second, his brain fogged, casting his mind back into the dark cloud of battle. Head on a swivel was a common phrase in the military that meant stay alert, danger was ever-present. But looking out at the Montana sky, he knew no danger was present. The Purple Heart Ranch was one of the safest places in the world, especially when it came to Wounded Warriors like him.

He didn't have to stay alert. He didn't have to stay on guard. The only conflict existed within him.

Linc tilted his head back. He let the tendons snap, crackle, and pop while he bathed in the rays of sunlight. The brightness of the light only barely penetrated the ever creeping darkness in his mind. Linc knew that pretty soon, the fog born of war, the shadows that had seeped into the corners of his brain and begun eating away at his attention, at his retention, that blackness would one day swallow him whole, leaving nothing behind.

The bark of a dog caught his attention. The tiny Irish Terrier looked up at him with large eyes on his small head. Its front paws pressed into the ground as though it stood at attention. It had no hind legs. Instead, there was a wheelchair attached to its limp back legs. The wheels came to a halt as the dog sat its rump on the ground.

Linc had to force himself to let out the breath he held as the dog sat. Many dogs in the military were trained to sit when they detected the chemicals that made up a bomb. But the dog in the wheelchair apparatus wouldn't have passed muster to be a field dog. Just as Linc no longer passed muster to operate in the field.

His operating days were over after the doctors

had operated on him. His body was whole, intact. It was his mind that was no longer cleared for duty.

Rolling his head again, Linc heard the tendons in his neck pop once more. The dog gave a pitying whine. Linc bent down and gave the pooch a scratch behind the ears. After the petting, the Terrier raised his rump and set his wheels in motion. Mission accomplished, he trotted off, having gotten what he came for.

Mission accomplished. Those words sounded like an echo in the hollow caverns of Linc's brain. He was supposed to be on a mission... but the details were hazy.

Linc rubbed at his brow, trying to remember what he'd come outside for? His duffel bag was at his feet, as though he were ready to be spun up and fly out to some distant land. There were car keys in one hand. He was cleared to operate an automobile, but he couldn't remember where he was meant to go?

Pressed into the flat of his palm behind the set of keys was a yellow square of paper. The adhesive at the top of the note stuck to the top of his palm. There were words scrawled across the center in a bold, blocky script.

Mission Objective: Silver Star Ranch.

Task: Keep Your Pledge to the General.

Linc's fogged mind cleared. Those words were enough to remind him of what he was meant to do, what his mission was, his final mission. He hefted up his duffel bag, clenched the car keys in his hands, and marched across the yard to the ranch's clinic.

Passing the nurses and doctors, Linc smiled blandly. It was hard for him to keep names and faces straight. These were the men and women who had helped him heal after his mission. He didn't want to appear rude to them. He wanted to appear healed. Though he would never truly be that again.

Reaching his destination, Linc didn't bother knocking on the door. It was ajar, and it was filled with five other men. One man sat on the bed. lacing up his boots. It was a slow-going job as he only used one hand for the job. Jefferson's left hand lay limp on the mattress as he struggled.

None of the other men made a move to help. None of them made it appear that they noticed the struggle. Jeff was the only one in their unit who'd walked away with a visible wound. The other men were able to hide their scars, but only if they didn't look each other in the eyes.

Once Jeff was finished, Linc asked, "Ready to go?"

Carter and Truman, the closest to the door nodding. Grabbing their duffels, they fell in with Lincoln. Wilson, who stood at the window, pushed off the wall. He reached for his duffel, and then for Jeff's before clenching his hand into a fist and drawing away. Jeff pretended not to notice and hefted the bag on his back with his right hand.

"We missed the funeral," said Jeff.

That couldn't be helped. They had all been laid up in a German hospital at the time of General Silver's funeral three months ago. Last month, they'd been sent to the Purple Heart Ranch to work on their internal wounds. Each man had balked at the idea of coming to the rehabilitation ranch. But it had been an order, the last edict of their commander in chief.

General Silver had been fond of calling his unit the President's Men because each of the soldiers had the name of a president. Linc had wondered if the general had handpicked the boys for that very reason. Whatever the general's selection process, it had been spot on. The six men had worked together seamlessly over the years, executing the toughest missions the military had thrown at them.

Until the last mission. The one that had nearly

taken their lives. The one that had cost them their most valuable player; the general himself.

"The Silver Star ranch is 312 clicks from here," Linc began. "We'll take two vehicles and drive out. We should arrive at 1100."

"This isn't a mission, Linc," said Wilson. "We're out of the military."

That was true. Each of the president's men had received a medical discharge after their time in the German hospital. Along with that honorable discharge, each man had received the Silver Medal of Honor for the heroic attempts they'd all undertaken in their last battle.

"All I want to do is rest," said Jackson. There was a touch of gray sneaking into the hairline at his temples.

"All I want to do is find a good woman and make some babies," said Carter as he ran a hand through his overly-styled hair.

Truman remained quiet. Like Linc, both of them wanted back in the military. But the only way that would happen is if they took a desk job. That was a slow death.

"We made a pledge to do this," said Linc.

That shut them up. Even three months later, they all still felt the loss of their leader acutely. Linc was sure each man could still hear the explosion that had taken their leader from them. All they had left of him was the pledge they'd made, the pledge to check in on his six daughters and see if there was anything that the President's Men could do for the girls.

"Let's gear up and roll out."

CHAPTER THREE

"Gunny, pick up," Scout hissed the order into the cell phone.

Normally, she was lucky to get three whole bars on the device. The service on the Silver Star Ranch was notoriously hit or miss. But it was a cloudless day. A flock of five birds flew in formation, mirroring the strong signal on the face of her phone. The only problem was the electronic chirping of the ring tone from the other end of the phone.

"Gunnery Ulysses Silver, you better pick up this phone or so help me—"

A long beep cut off Scout's threat to her sister. Scout yanked the phone from her ear and glared at the device. With a huff, she hit redial.

"I know you're there," Scout huffed into the

receiver. In response, the phone rang and rang again. "They get cell service out in the middle of...where is she again?"

"The Namib Desert," said Brig as she led a tall Thoroughbred to the slow feeder.

The once-proud racehorse walked slowly on the lead, his head hanging low. Scout winced as she watched the horse's large, soulful brown gaze narrow as though each step were painful.

They probably were. Heathcliff had come to them after losing his tenth consecutive race two years ago. His owner had been fed up and ready to put the horse down now that he was no longer profitable. Scout had convinced the wretched man to give the horse to her. She and Saylor had slowly nursed the weary horse back to some semblance of health, though he would never race again. Which was for the best.

No one here would try to coax any horse to be all it could be. Only to be what they were. The Silver Star Ranch was a place of rehabilitation, of reform, maybe even a bit of revitalization. But not restoration.

The horses that came here had been broken, either in body or spirit, by the humans who had owned them. Scout had no interest in patching them up and sending them back. Here the animals would live out the rest of their days at peace as they healed from the inside out.

Originally, this had been a working cattle ranch. But on her twenty-first birthday, just three years after her mother's passing, and her father's continual absence as he took on mission after mission with the military, Scout had sold off the cattle and transformed the land into a rehabilitation ranch for retired and abused horses.

Her father had balked at the idea, insisting she would fail. He'd also insisted it was high time she got married and let a man run the ranch for her. She'd told him that if he wanted a man in charge, then he could come home and run the place himself.

He hadn't come home. Their calls became fewer and further between. Until there were none, and he was gone.

Scout sniffed and rubbed at her nose. She blinked a couple of times, trying to clear whatever dust was in the air. The bleep of the voice message indicator rang in her ear, announcing that her sister would not be taking her call anytime soon.

Scout had the urge to slam the phone down. But she didn't dare. She didn't want to startle the magnificent creature on her own lead. And so she disconnected the call and turned to a problem she could solve.

Bingley had chunks missing out of his blond hide. A result of getting caught in a wire fence for hours. The Sorrel horse was still a beautiful animal with its flaxen coat and mane. Because of its coloring, the Silver sisters had named it after the equally flaxen hero of their mother's favorite novel.

"Don't worry, boy," Scout soothed. "I'll figure it out. I won't let anyone take any of us from our home."

Bingley pawed the ground. He shook his head back and forth, a low whine escaping his mouth. Scout wondered if he doubted her? It was more likely the horse's deep-seated distrust of humans. He'd been badly treated. The gashes in his skin had come from the neglect of his former owners. The wires had dug deep and held fast for hours before anyone had noticed.

Even today, the animal startled easily when it felt confined and cornered. Both Brig and Scout made sure to keep in the horse's eyesight as they tended his wounds, wounds they'd have to tend for the rest of the horse's natural life. The owners had discarded the animal when he had lost his looks.

But to Scout's eyes, the male was still beautiful with his healed scars.

All of the two dozen horses on this ranch had stolen into Scout's heart over the years. She and her sisters had been the ones to nurse each and every one of them out of the dark and back into the light. They had given love and attention, kindness, and care when the ones who had originally taken on the job had turned their backs.

And now her father thought he could force his daughters' hands? Do away with all the good they'd done all because he never got the son he craved. Not if she had anything to do about it.

But what could she do about it? Father Matthews had shown her how the paperwork was all there. There were no loopholes. Either she and her sisters got married, or they'd lose it all.

"Gunny said she would be out of pocket for at least a month," said Brig.

They didn't have that much time. Already two weeks had passed since the reading of their dad's will. They only had a few months left before the end of the year. And none of his daughters had any prospect of marriage. Except for Mareen.

Mareen was scheduled to have a winter wedding just before Christmas. Scout only knew because she'd seen the announcement in the society papers. None of her sisters had received an invitation.

What Scout was more surprised by was that the wedding was still on. She wouldn't put it past Cruella to push the wedding back a few weeks so that the ranch would come to her. But she supposed her stepmother knew her ex-husband's daughters too well. She knew that there was no way the five opinionated, loud-mouthed, unfinished girls could land a man in three years, let alone three months.

Rehabilitating these animals had become Scout's life work; Saylor's too. They weren't going to give it up because of a man. All she had to do was find a husband. How hard could that be? People married every day. And divorced the next day—if her family was any example.

However, Scout was having problems finding a man to leg shackle. She wasn't exactly sure where to go about finding one for herself? None of the boys in town would do. She'd grown up with them. Beat them at one too many sports. Raised her hand to answer every question they got wrong. Surprisingly, boys didn't like that.

Maybe she should go out of town? But where would she go when she got there? A bar? She wasn't much of a drinker. A night club? She was even less of a dancer. And she had nothing to wear.

What was her father thinking? It's not like men fell out of the sky.

The sound of boots on the ground had Scout turning around. Walking up to the fence where six of the tallest, broadest men she'd ever seen in her life. The one in the lead was a beautiful specimen.

He wasn't the tallest. The brown-skinned man at his left had a few inches on him. But the guy at the center had a larger than life air about him. His dark gaze was clear, focused. The pectorals of his broad chest were clearly defined by the tan shirt he wore. Resting against the center of his chest was the unmistakable rectangle of dog tags.

Soldiers.

What were soldiers doing on her ranch? What were six soldiers doing on her ranch? Right after the reading of her father's will and the crazy edict he'd laid out for his six daughters?

Bingley must have had the same tingling of suspicion race across his back because he pawed at the ground some more. His head shook more forcefully in the lead. He couldn't see the threat that was coming at his flank.

Before Scout could grab her wits, the horse

reared up on its hind legs. Bingley broke free and took off. Scout's feet were slow as she made to scramble after Bingley. But apparently, there was no need as the six soldiers entered the enclosure and spread out around the horse.

CHAPTER FOUR

*L*inc hadn't grown up with horses. None of the President's Men had. But when they'd become a unit under the General, it was one of the first things Silver had insisted his men learn; how to ride but also how to manage a horse.

"In a herd, there's always a passive leader, and there is always an alpha leader," General Silver was fond of saying. "The alpha horse is warm-blooded and bossy. They'll push and shove their way to the front. The other horses will get out of their way, but rarely do you see them follow the alpha."

When that mighty blond horse reared up on its hind legs, Linc didn't need to call out an order. He silently, slowly moved into the enclosure. His men fanned out behind him, following in his footsteps.

"The passive leader concerns himself with the herd," General Silver had taught them. "They are watchful of events and will stand by if another horse is separated or in distress. It is for this mindset of unity and egalitarianism that other horses willingly follow them."

When the blond horse had startled, it had nearly knocked over the woman who held it's lead. In that instant, Linc's full attention switched from the troubled horse to the woman.

It was her eyes. Even from yards away, the brilliance of their blue struck him. Linc's shoulders snapped straight when that startling gaze settled on him. He had the drive to rear up onto his toes and paw at the ground at the sight of her. He wanted to growl gleefully in the air to all around him. He wanted to follow her around the enclosure until he had her full attention.

But something was blocking his way to her. It was the tetchy, blond horse that was now loose. Linc had wanted to spring into action and head straight for the blue-eyed angel. He almost had. It was Jefferson's hand on his shoulder that held him back.

Linc had nearly forgotten the General's training. You never charged a nervous horse. Only an alpha would make such a foolish move. You approached the horse calmly, quietly, passively, letting it see that you meant it no harm.

Without a word spoken, the six soldiers spread out around the enclosure. Slowly, quietly, calmly. From the corner of his eyes, Linc could see that even their breaths were in sync. The President's Men moved as a unit toward the beast, cutting off any route of escape.

The horse slowed its nervous motions, but it didn't stop. Its head swayed right and left, a sign that it was still anxious. Jefferson's voice rose up. His tones calm and soothing.

"Lower you heard, boy," Jeff said. He lifted his right hand, his left arm hanging limp at his side. "It's all right. We're friends."

As if in a trance, the horse began to heed Jeff's command. Linc took the opportunity to sidestep that action and move around the horse to the woman the horse had broke from.

For the first time, Linc noticed there were actually two women. Neither had moved from their spots at the far side of the enclosure. They both stared, blue eyes agape at the six men surrounding their horse. It was clear these were two of the general's daughters. If not for the brown hair and proud chins, it would be the blue eyes that told him. Linc had never seen another shade like it.

He did a quick visual check of the woman on the other side of the fence. She was younger, a bit of youthful roundness still clung to her cheeks. Her shock was quickly wearing off to be replaced by amusement and something akin to devilry, a look the general used to get in his eyes before calling an audible change in the mission plan.

Linc's gaze skated past the younger Silver to the woman inside the enclosure. Once again, his gaze found hers and held. And held.

The constant fog that had settled around Linc's head since that last op dissipated and cleared as he looked down into her clear blue gaze. With the fog of war gone, everything made sense to him again. All of his thoughts fell into alignment. All of the tracks of his understanding and reasoning synched up and arrowed at her.

Linc's hand itched for his pen and sticky notes. He wanted to be sure he didn't forget anything about her. Not the fact of the tilt at the corner of her right eyelash. Not the notion that her nostrils flared as she exhaled. Not the matter of how the center-left of her lush lips pursed as she took his measure.

He stood at attention for her. His shoulders were

back. His chin was high. But he didn't avert his gaze as he'd been taught at the military academy. No, he looked directly into that blue gaze, hoping he passed muster, while he waited for any order she might give. Because he knew, without question, that he'd take on any mission this breathtaking creature assigned him.

"Who are you?" she demanded. Her voice was haughty. Her words clipped. Her tone demanded an answer.

Linc couldn't hide the smile that split his face. She was definitely the General's daughter. Likely the eldest. What was her name? He knew the General had told him. He'd told them all his daughters' names. But the details weren't ones that Linc kept at the top of his list of sticky notes.

"Your father sent me," he said.

At that, her gaze narrowed even further on him. That right eyelash lifting higher. "Let me guess; he sent you to marry me."

That had not been the reason for the mission here. Had it? Linc wanted to consult his notes.

He sent you to marry me.

Linc didn't feel the need to reach into his pocket. His mind was clear. His synapses were firing. In fact, they were rewriting his purpose for being here, on this ranch, in real-time. Across the front of his brain, Linc saw a new web of objectives and tasks arranging themselves. His new mission objective was clear as the light of day, clear as the blue of her gaze.

He sent you to marry me.

Lincoln Rawlings was a soldier first and foremost. He was a man who lived for the next mission. His commander had sent him here as his final mission. But General Silver had not been clear on his objective as he lay dying from his injuries.

He sent you to marry me.

Linc wouldn't need a reminder that this is what he was meant to do with his life. General Silver's daughter's features were burned into every part of his brain, including the parts that weren't working optimally. More importantly, her suggestion was a command he wanted to follow. A mission he was eager to take on. A task he was already tactically preparing for.

He sent you to marry me.

That hadn't exactly been the General's last edict to his men, but every part of Linc was happy to follow this order.

CHAPTER FIVE

"Lincoln Rawlings, ma'am."

It was just three words, but Scout heard the lazy Southern drawl in them. The sound sent a shiver across her shoulder blades. The tall, broad soldier dipped his head, more like a Victorian gentleman would've done in a ballroom upon meeting a young debutant.

Scout was no such flowery miss. So she wasn't sure why her hand raised, knuckles up, as though she were expecting a kiss, instead of palm out, as though she was expecting a quick handshake.

"Scout Silver," she announced, leaving her hand the way it was and waiting in breathless anticipation to see what he would do with her offering.

Lincoln Rawlings didn't disappoint. He took her

fingers in his. He didn't lift her hand and bring her knuckles to his lips for a light kiss. Nor did he turn her palm over and crush her fingers in a rough handshake to prove his manliness.

His pinky was the first to make impact. The smallest of his digits spanned the length of her entire hand. That first finger curled at the base of her fingers, just under the webbing where the top of her palm met the calluses just below four of her digits.

Next came his ring finger, which Scout had the presence of mind to notice that it was, in fact, ringless. His middle finger was long enough to wrap around the outside of her thumb. His index finger curled up in a come hither motion as it connected with her own index finger. But he was not done.

His thumb brushed over the back of her hand. It gently caressed the harsh hills of her knuckles until it came to settle in the fleshy valley between her index finger and thumb, making a loop with his own index finger.

This was worse than a gripping handshake. This was better than a courtly brush of lips. Scout felt pulled to this man, lassoed with the ropes coming taut around her. She felt herself coming to heel. She felt herself wanting to follow his lead.

With that last thought, she snatched her hand away from him. Lincoln Rawlings let her go with no resistance. Scout hid her hand behind her back, as though it was a separate entity from her. All the while, the heat he'd ignited with his touch spread like wildfire up her arm and throughout her entire body.

"Scout?" Lincoln said with a grin. "Right, I remember now. You're just as your father described you."

Part of Scout wanted to reject that notion; the idea of her father speaking about any of his daughters for any reason. When he was away, which was most of the time, he treated them as though they didn't exist.

But then there was the other part of her, the part that wanted to know everything her father had said about her to this man. Had he spoken of her in a proud manner? Did he tell Lincoln about her accomplishments? Had he known about her accomplishments? He couldn't have. She'd stopped bothering to tell him years ago. It wasn't like he showed up for any of them.

"Tall, long mane of hair," Lincoln was saying, "and long legs like a colt."

Scout bristled at that. Her father had called her

his little colt when she was a child. But that was many years ago. She wasn't sure if she liked Lincoln Rawlings thinking of her as a gangly-legged pony.

"We were his unit." Lincoln spread his arms to encompass the other five men.

Four of the men were resting hips and shoulders against the fence. They all stood, partly watching Lincoln and Scout as they talked, partly watching as the fifth man led Bingley around the enclosure. The horse was calm on the lead, not pulling or even swaying his head.

Scout noted that the man who held the reins was only using one arm to do so. The other hung unnaturally limp at his side. She didn't stare. She had better manners and had seen worse injuries.

"That's Jefferson with the horse," Lincoln said. "And this is Wilson, Jackson, Carter, and Truman."

"Nice to meet you." That came from Brig. "I'm Brigadear."

Brig had tied up Heathcliff and was leaning against the other side of the fence nearest the men. The girl always had been boy crazy. Brig's gaze lingered on the dark-skinned man who stood at the edge of the bunch. There was a touch of gray just above his ear, though he didn't look much older than Scout.

Scout would be the first to admit that the Silver sisters had daddy issues. But Brig seemed to tend toward men who were a bit too old for her. Each of her crushes had always been on her male teachers and not on the boys sitting next to her, jockeying for her attention.

Scout made it a point to glare at the older man; Jackson had been the name Lincoln had called him. For his part, Jackson gave a shake of his head and stepped back from Brig.

"Hey, wait," said Brig, "aren't all those names of the U.S. Presidents?"

"Yup," said the man Lincoln had pointed out as Carter. "Your dad was fond of calling us the President's Men."

"That's cute," Brig said, but her gaze skated past the young Carter with his sculpted hair and landed back on Jackson.

"Funny how you six show up so soon after the reading of my father's will," said Scout.

"We're sorry we couldn't get here sooner," said Lincoln in that sultry voice of his. His gaze was cast down, as though in shame. "Your father made his men pledge that, should he die in combat, to check on his daughters at the Silver Star Ranch, and see if they needed anything."

"How convenient," Scout scoffed as she made her way over to Jefferson and Bingley. She took the reins from the man and turned to lead the horse to the fence. As she did, she looked the six men up and down again.

These were exactly the kinds of men his father wanted for sons. Loyal soldiers, following his orders without question. That hadn't worked so well when her father had produced wily daughter after daughter. So this was his plan to finally get his daughters to heel, marrying these six men and put the ranch in their control.

She could see the general's signature all over this. A contingency plan in case he died. Six husbands for his daughters.

Fat chance that would work. Even if Lincoln was the walking epitome of everything that Scout found attractive in a man. She would never marry him for the sole reason of him being her father's choice.

But at the same time, he was her only choice if she wanted to save the ranch. Could she go through with a marriage to a man set up by the father who had abandoned her?

"We're here at your convenience," Lincoln was saying. "We've all recently separated from the service after..."

Lincoln looked away from her. His mouth shut, and his hazel gaze darkened. It was as though a storm cloud moved in in real-time. Scout had the urge to turn his face back to hers and wipe the look away.

"We have some downtime," said Jefferson, coming to stand beside Lincoln. "We figured we'd come here and help out around the ranch in any way you need."

"In honor of my father's last request?" said Scout.

Lincoln turned back to her. The fog in his gaze lifted. "Yes, ma'am. Anything you girls need. We owe it to the general. We gave our word. A soldier's word is his bond."

Not for all soldiers. But fine. Scout had some jobs that they could do around the ranch while she decided whether or not they passed muster for the job she needed them for most.

CHAPTER SIX

*S*crape. *Whoosh. Thud.*

The sound of the metal tines hitting the dirt over and over again was surprisingly soothing to Linc. The scent of manure in the air wasn't that much of a bother. The clunking sound the heaps made when sent the heaps into the trash can was oddly satisfying.

"I'm sure this isn't what the General had in mind when he told us to check on his daughters," Carter grumbled.

Scrape. Whoosh. Splat.

Carter dropped his shovel to the ground with a yelp. He lifted the toe of his designer cowboy boots for inspection. "Man, I got horse droppings on my boot."

Linc turned from the male and continued his work. For a man who had crawled through a field of bloodied bodies slogged through the harsh jungle, and even waded bobbing refuse, Carter was extremely fastidious when he was out of fatigues.

The six of them were fresh-faced, well-rested, and up at the crack of dawn. Linc had woken confused in the small log cabin behind the main house of the ranch. But after he'd looked over on the nightstand at the note he'd left himself, his mind instantly cleared.

He'd been looking at that note for months. This morning he was able to check off the first tick on his mission objectives. Reaching for the pen next to the stack of stickies, he put a bold checkmark next to the words Pass Patton.

General Silver had been fond of naming each step of a mission objective or task after other generals and military figures of history. The Patton Objective was the first phase of this mission. They'd arrived at the Silver Star Ranch and met the general's daughters. But somehow Linc knew, their work here wasn't done.

Next objective; Stonewall. He needed to find out what Scout Silver was hiding. Because he knew she was hiding something behind those bright blue eyes. But he had no idea what it could be or how to break past her defenses.

"Does anyone else feel like we walked into a trap?" Truman yanked a length of rope from the tack wall and set about rewrapping it. He made concise circles, but he winced each time he brought the rope up to his shoulder.

Linc's brain focused on the man's wince. The synapses in his brain misfired a few times before the connection was made. Truman pinned down under a heavy pillar, a fallen wall. The man's left hand empty of the sniper rifle always at his side. That was the last time Linc remembered seeing Truman lift a weapon.

"Marriage?" said Truman. "You heard her say that, right?"

Linc's mind traveled back to yesterday. The sight of Scout Silver standing in the sunlight was as clear as a new day in his usually foggy brain.

He sent you to marry me.

Linc had not forgotten those words. They'd played the rest of the day and into the night on a loop inside his head. That was part of his Stonewall Objective; to find out what Scout Silver meant when she'd said those words.

"Didn't we escape all that nonsense by leaving

the Purple Heart Ranch," Truman was saying. Marriage was the last thing the man wanted. What Truman wanted was for his shoulder to heal properly and to get back into active duty.

For himself, Linc knew that active duty was no longer in question. Not with the lag time in his thinking and the constant tangle of his thoughts. He was grounded for the rest of his life. What he would do with it, he had no idea.

"Do you really think the general would've wanted any of us for his daughters?"

Linc wasn't sure who'd spoken. Often if he wasn't giving his full attention, he missed these kinds of details. What he was more interested in focusing on was the question itself.

"General Silver was a smart man." Those placating tones were all Wilson. "He was a brilliant tactician who was always two and three steps ahead of the enemy."

"These aren't the enemy," Carter piped in. "They're his daughters."

"Right, his daughters." The cynicism in Truman's voice was hard to mistake. "Who he told us all about."

A large part of their job as soldiers was to hurry up and wait. In those long, waiting hours, the

General would share stories about his daughters. Linc knew a lot about Scout. He knew she rescued horses. He knew Saylor was a vet who specialized in large animals; a livestock veterinarian he thought it was called. He'd heard tales of Mareen Silver winning medals in dressage, though Linc still wasn't clear on what that was. Something or other about horse dancing. He knew the twins had done horse vaulting, which he'd figured was akin to gymnastics on a horse. And the youngest, Brig was studying equine therapy at college.

"Then he made us promise to come here in the case of his death," Truman went on. "And the first thing out of his eldest daughter's mouth was marriage."

He sent you to marry me.

Linc shook the thought from his head. "None of us are fit for a wife."

It was true. The blast that had taken the General from them had left wounds too deep to heal any time soon. Definitely too deep to bring a woman into any of their spheres. But even as he thought of all the negatives, the possibility of it thrilled Linc.

He sent you to marry me.

Linc had no trouble remembering each of those words. The flare of her nostrils as she said them.

The pull at the corner of her eyes as she'd sized him up.

Had that been hope in her blue eyes? Had it been anger? He couldn't be sure.

"But I'm happy to do any work we can for these girls," said Linc. "It's the least we can do for them."

A silent agreement settled in the barn. They each knew why it was the least of things. Because they had failed to do one thing. They'd failed to save the girls' father. If that mission hadn't gone wrong, the general might be here now mucking out these stalls himself.

Linc lifted his gaze as a truck ambled down the road. Two women hopped out to unlatch the gate. When the gate swung inward, he saw the silver star emblem of the ranch. It still galled Linc when he thought about the honor ceremony where they'd each received the Silver Star Medal. The medal was for their bravery in that last mission. Brave they'd been, but the mission had not been accomplished. They'd lost their commander. They'd each lost a part of themselves.

Linc turned his attention back to the horses. At least this was one mess that he could clean up. He'd only make a mess if he even thought about anything more than his duty to Scout Silver.

Linc caught a heap of manure up into his shovel and tossed it. The movements were practiced ones from his time at the Purple Heart Ranch. He'd loved working with the horses there. They were uncomplicated animals. They didn't require words to understand them. He need only look into their eyes and see what they needed.

The horse in the back stall stuck his head out. It had a dark mane of hair that was the color of midnight. But its large eyes were brown and fathomless.

No. Not fathomless. Linc saw confusion in those depths. He watched the horse gaze around at the walls confining him and then lower his head. The magnificent beast pawed at the ground and shook his head from side to side as though in a panic at the confinement.

Linc didn't think. He reacted. He dropped his shovel and went to the stall.

The gold plate on the stall read Wickham. Linc put his hand out to the horse. Wickham backed up. His ears went flat to his neck, a sure sign of aggression.

Linc held still, breathing calmly in and out, and waited. It took a few tense moments, but slowly the horse's ears relaxed. It took first one, then another tentative step toward him. Wickham dipped his head, as though sniffing Linc's palm like a dog would a new friend.

Apparently, Linc passed muster for the horse. Wickham nudged Linc's hand up and onto his long nose. Linc obliged, patting the horse's muzzle. Even being so bold as to scratch behind the horse's ears, which didn't flatten again.

Wickham raised his soulful gaze to Linc. The communication between man and horse was clear. The horse needed to get out of this confinement. He needed some space to roam. Linc understood the sentiment perfectly.

CHAPTER SEVEN

"Who called the hot guy brigade?" asked Tilly as she tossed her bag down on the kitchen counter. Her blonde hair hung down in lush waves over her shoulders as her blue eyes widened to take in the sight out the back window.

Saylor, who was on Tilly's heels, had her head craned over one shoulder like an owl trying to determine if it had found a new sparkly treasure or if there was danger afoot. "Are they here for lessons? Or... something?"

Saylor's brown tresses were pulled back into an orderly queue that rested between her shoulder blades. Those blades were tense at the same time as they sagged forward. It hadn't escaped Scout that her sister hadn't come home last night.

"They're not here for lessons," said Scout. "But they are here for something."

She stood at the large picture window in the kitchen that sat over the huge farmhouse sink. Saylor came up to her right shoulder, Tilly came to stand at her left. Brig stood on tippy toes to look over Scout's shoulder.

"Well?" said Tilly. "What are they here for?"

The men in question had been set to mucking out the horse stalls when they woke at the crack of dawn this morning. Scout had startled to see them coming out of the cabins that arced around the big house.

There were six cabins. The General had had one built for each of his daughters on their thirteenth birthdays. It had never occurred to him to wait until the more monumental sixteenth birthday. Nor did the idea of jewelry or a car ever enter his strategic mind.

No, General Silver felt that the pinnacle year of any child's life was when they turned thirteen. And homeownership was his idea of a meaningful gift. In his defense, each of his daughters had a pony before they could walk.

"The General sent them," said Scout.

"Sent them for what?" asked Saylor.

"He sent them to marry us," Brig squealed behind Scout's ear.

Scout ducked her head just in time for the barrage of sonic sounds to assault her. There was Brig still squealing her eagerness. There was Tilly's shriek of indignance at their father's heavy-handedness. There was Saylor's blaring silence as her gaze swung from the window to Scout and back again.

The six men were out of the barn. They lined their shovels up against the wall, just like toy soldiers. Scout didn't doubt that the interior of the structure would be entirely spotless. They were the General's men, and she knew first hand that General Silver did not suffer uncleanliness.

What she wasn't expecting was for a couple of the men to remove their shirts from their bodies to wipe the sweat from their brows and neck. Lincoln Rawlings was one of the strippers.

Her ears were ringing. But not from her sisters' chatterboxes. Each Silver sister was quiet as they took in the scene of bare, man flesh before them.

Muscles. Lots of muscles. Biceps glistening in the late morning sun. Chests rising and sinking with deep breaths and gulps of the lemonade Brig had set out earlier. A few pats on the back, as though for a job well done, but more than likely for a well-delivered jab between friends. And then, the kicker.

Lincoln Rawlings smiled. Grinned was more like it. That's when the morning shifted to afternoon, and the sun shone brightly in the sky. So bright that the rays passed through the glass of the kitchen window and warmed Scout all the way through.

"Dad sent us a squad of men?" said Tilly, all hints of indignation had slipped from her voice.

"Hmmm," hummed Brig.

"They said they're here to marry us?" said Saylor, her shoulders now straight.

"Hmmm," repeated Brig.

"No, they didn't say that," said Scout. "But the timing of it..."

"You think dad planned this?" said Tilly.

"Wouldn't be the first time the General tried to move his family around on a chessboard."

"I'll marry one," said Brig, raising her hand.

"You are not getting married," said Scout. "You're too young."

"I'm a college senior," Brig countered. "And besides, if we don't do this, then we lose the ranch."

Scout pinched her earlobe. She caught sight of

Lincoln dipping back into the barn. As he went, he pulled his shirt back over his head. Scout sighed... in relief, of course. Barns were messy places, and she didn't want to be responsible for dry cleaning.

"I'd never marry a soldier," Tilly was saying.

"But you'd marry a Russian mobster," said Scout.

"Sergei is not a mobster."

"Where's his picture."

Tilly pinched her lips together in the way she'd done since she was three when she was trying to explain her child logic to an adult.

"Ordering up a male order, Russian groom is not how we're going to deal with this either." Scout put force into her voice. But she was dealing with one of General Silver's daughters.

Though she pitied any scam artist who thought they could worm their way into this family, she kinda hoped one would try. The Silver sisters had terrorized the valley for years. Teachers groaned when they learned they'd have one in their classrooms. Coaches' hair turned gray when they learned one of the girls might be on their team for the season. Heaven help them if they had to deal with two at a time.

"I promised I'd get married. It's not like I have to stay married. Our parents certainly didn't."

But that's not how Scout wanted to treat a marriage. She wanted to get into a relationship and stay there. Just like this had been her home all her life, she didn't want to bounce around in a relationship.

"Well, I certainly don't need to marry one of them," said Saylor.

The three sisters turned away from the window and looked at her. Really looked at her. The tension in Saylor's shoulders was gone, but she wasn't relaxed. She was never relaxed. Looking into her eyes, Scout could always see the truth.

The bags under her eyes weren't going down, letting Scout know that she'd faced another sleepless night last evening. Her blue eyes were red and puffy, not shining and bright. What had that creep done now?

"Nick is thinking about proposing," said Saylor. Her voice didn't go shrill with delight. It wobbled with uncertainty.

"He said that?" asked Tilly.

"Well, I brought it up, and he didn't shoot it down. So..." Saylor let that linger, her gaze on the ground.

"So, he's thinking about it," said Brig. Her tone was a clear attempt to be helpful to her older sister, but the hard glint in her blue eyes gave credence to what Tilly and Scout were both thinking.

Nick was Saylor's first boyfriend. Though it had taken him years of clandestine dating before he allowed her to call him that. Years while he was dating other girls right under Saylor's nose. But just like now, Saylor's gaze was down on the floor. Scout hated that her sister thought she only deserved the scraps on the floor.

Maybe marrying one of the guys outside wasn't such a bad idea. Especially if Scout could thrust Saylor onto one of them. But not Lincoln. Maybe the soft-spoken Jefferson who had been so good with her horse the other day.

Lincoln was walking back out of the barn. But he wasn't alone. He had a horse on a lead. A dark horse who was already starting to tug.

"Scout, what's wrong? Your face just went pale?"

"It's Wickham."

CHAPTER EIGHT

When Linc had stepped out of the sun and back into the barn, the dimness of the space had confused him. The sticky note at the top of his post-its gave the objective to clean the stalls. But looking around, they were already mucked. So what was he doing back in here?

At the back of the barn, he heard a pitiful whinny. The fog cleared from Linc's brain and his steps became purposeful. He marched to the back and up to the horse.

William? No, Wickham was the name emblazoned in the door to the horse's quarters. Linc felt like he should know that name, but he didn't want to press his brain too hard. He'd completed the task given to him this morning by Scout, but he wanted to do more.

After giving Wickham a reassuring pat on the muzzle, Linc turned to the tack wall. He'd had Truman organize the equipment there into a more logical array. They'd hung saddles and bridles up on the wall instead of posting them on the portable saddle racks. Now there was more space on the floor. They'd added more hooks to hang halters, crops, reins, and girths. He'd made a note to build some wall-hanging cabinets for additional storage.

With his way cleared, Linc reached for a halter. Turning back to Wickham, he held up the device. The horse's large eyes caught sight of the halter and bowed its head. Clearly, Wickham wanted to be out and free for a spell. Linc doubted Scout would mind. It would be another thing off her to-do list if he gave this antsy horse a bit of exercise.

As soon as the door to the stall opened, the seemingly charming horse reared up.

Linc knew better than to panic and try to pull down or step back. Instead, he loosened the reins and stood his ground. The blast from that fatal mission had left his brain foggy and unable to hold normal processes in his head. But when it came to horses, it was all instinctual.

He knew that Wickham was trying to show dominance. The horse was clearly an alpha male. But so was Linc.

After Wickham reared and his front hooves landed back on the ground, Linc pulled down on the ropes of the halter. With the horse's muzzle down, Linc advanced, causing the horse to take several steps back. It also established exactly which alpha was in control.

They stood there like that for several moments. Staring each other down. Once Linc was sure man and beast had an understanding, he led the horse out of the barn.

Wickham stayed in step with Linc as he took one turn around the enclosure. Satisfied by this behavior, Linc brought the horse over for a visit with the men. He could positively feel the horse's delight at being amongst the other males. Horses were, after all, herd animals. They didn't like to be separated from their pack. It was clear Wickham wanted to be apart of the President's Men.

"Stop what you're doing."

Lincoln gripped the reins tight as he turned to the sound of that voice. There was the timbre of her father in Scout Silver's voice. But just a timbre. There was still a healthy helping of the feminine in that sultry voice. It sent a shiver up and down Linc's spine until it came to settle somewhere in his chest.

"He's dangerous," said Scout.

"Who? Wickham?" Lincoln frowned. "Nah, he's pretty well behaved."

Of course, at that moment, Linc felt the horse's head preparing to jerk as though he was going to rear up again. Before Wickham could misbehave and prove him wrong, Linc gave a yank down on the ropes in his hand. The horse sighed in submission, like a child whose parent yanked his hand away from the cookie jar before he could reach in.

Scout pursed her lips at the two of them. Clearly, she'd seen the dominance play. Her gaze on the horse was one of disappointment. Wickham had the presence of mind to focus his large eyes down on the ground.

Scout's look at Linc was a cross between exasperation and bewilderment. He gathered the poor woman wasn't sure what to do with him.

"He's not usually good with people," she said, giving the horse another assessing glance.

"Neither am I these days," said Linc. "But I think we understand each other."

Now Scout's assessing gaze was back on Linc.

Linc wanted to understand her. He wanted Scout to understand him.

"That's enough recreation for now," she said. "Mr. Wickham needs to be put up. He's on a schedule."

"Yes, ma'am."

Scout allowed Linc to lead Wickham back into the barn. She was close on their heels. So when she gasped, Linc heard the intake of breath.

"What have you done in here?" she asked, her eyes fixed on the tack wall.

"Just organized things," Linc said as he led Wickham back into his stall and shut the horse in. "Is it not to your liking? I can change it."

"No," she whispered, her hand grazing over the hanging saddles. "No, it's... perfect. It makes sense to have everything just as you've arranged it. It's exactly what I didn't know I needed."

Linc's chest puffed up at her praise. He wondered what else she didn't know she needed. He was determined to find out. That was still his mission. He wanted to pass Stonewall. He wanted to find out what she was hiding so that he could be the one to give her what she needed. Everything seemed clear when he was looking into her eyes. He wished he could do it every day for the rest of his life; have the clarity he saw when he looked at her.

"Why are you really here?" she said.

"I told you; your father sent me."

"What for?"

"For whatever you need."

Linc pushed off the door to Wickham's stall. He stepped toward Scout. He held out his hands, worried that she would rear back. She didn't. Like the alpha mare that she was, she held her ground.

"You really don't know?" she said. "Do you?"

He shook his head. But whatever it was, Linc wanted to know. Instead of asking, Linc held his tongue and remained silent. He found that often worked best when he wasn't certain what he should be doing or how he should be responding.

"This is my home," she said. "It's always been my home. I don't want to leave it."

"Why would you have to? Are you having money troubles? I can help—"

"No. I'm not...anymore. It was hard after my parent's second divorce. But my sisters and I turned this place around. It's not making a huge profit, but it's enough to pay the bills and send Brig to school."

"Then what? What do you need."

"Why did he send you?"

Now it was Linc who swallowed. Could she see through him? Did she know their failure to her father? The military had called them heroes, given them medals. But not a single man that served her father felt deserving of those honors.

"He sent me to take care of anything you need. Is there something you need, Scout?"

"Yeah." Her chin jutted up in the same way her father's would when his superiors questioned his strategy. "I need a husband."

The admission didn't shock him. It was kinda hard to shock a man whose brain fogged over most of the day. Somehow, Lincoln felt he'd known this all along. This had been his objective in coming here. He'd just passed Objective Stonewall.

"My dad put in his will that each of his daughters has to get married within the year, or the ranch goes to his remaining ex-wife. Cruella—I mean Catherine— hates this ranch and will sell it the first chance she gets."

Lincoln moved closer, the need to protect this woman overwhelming him. For some reason, the love story of George and Martha Washington came to his mind. The two had doted on one another and been nearly inseparable their whole marriage.

"With you all coming here, on the General's orders, so soon after his death, I just thought..."

Scout's gaze lifted to his. The blue was so vibrant

that everything else around him paled to shades of dull gray. The idea of catching her, saddling her with a ring on her finger, and leading her through these pastures for the rest of his life was all his mind could wrap around.

"You think he sent me here to marry you?" said Linc.

Scout nodded.

The very thought of having a new person in his life, having to learn their patterns when his mind could barely hold onto the processes in his past, should've sent Linc into a panic. But the idea of marriage to this woman felt like the most natural thing in the world.

"Okay," he said.

Scout finally took a step back. "Okay?"

"Yes, okay." He took a step toward her. When she didn't rear back, he continued. "I'll marry you."

"You'll...marry...me?"

"If it will help you keep this place that you love, if it'll help keep you safe, then yes."

The mission specs were forming in Linc's mind. To fulfill the General's dying wish, he needed to protect his daughters. To do that, he needed to protect the ranch. To do that, he needed to marrying Scout.

He saw no hardship in this new objective, the Washington Objective.

"Yes?" Scout frowned. "Why?"

Because he felt grounded near her. Because he had already memorized every line of her face. Because the sound of her voice cleared the fog in his brain.

"Because I owe your father."

CHAPTER NINE

"You cannot marry him." Tilly threw her hands up. When she did, flakes of white flour rained down, mixing in with her blonde curls, making her look like a Christmas angel. "You just met him."

"I think it's romantic," said Brig, dipping a finger into the cake mix instead of the wooden stirring spoon. She brought her finger and the sweet batter into her mouth but still managed to clearly say, "Like something out of a Hallmark movie."

"I don't have many options," Scout said as she opened the oven door to check the roast. Just another minute and the meat would be ready to fall off the bones. "We're running out of time."

"I still think we can contest the general's will,"

said Saylor from the other end of the kitchen. Her back was against a wall as she tossed a bright salad of lettuce, tomatoes, and cucumbers.

They'd already been over the will with a lawyer and a fine-tooth comb. Granted, the lawyer they'd hired had been off a late-night TV ad. And he hadn't taken their call the first couple of times, thinking their case was a prank. And also that he'd laughed, rather unprofessionally, when he'd finally gone over the paperwork. Only to deliver the news that the document would hold up in a court of law.

Either each Silver sister gets married to retain her rights to the land, or the ranch goes to their stepmother.

Scout could still remember the first time Cruella had come to the ranch. Each of her footsteps had been light, careful, as though she were certain she'd step on horse droppings even when she stood in the family room. Her nose had been turned up at the same time her lips had been turned down, as though she smelled something foul as dinner roasted in the oven.

Catherine Chesterfield Silver had hated this place and wanted to leave the moment she came here. She hadn't come back, but she'd left her mark.

She'd urged the General to turn the ranch into something useful, like an exclusive resort.

Just the thought made Scout shudder. The sound of her sisters' bickering brought her back to the present reality. Tilly swatted at Brig's hand as she tried to swipe another taste of cake mix. Saylor wiped at the flour on Brig's cheek before their youngest sister could get away from the maternal care.

This wasn't an exclusive resort for the rich and dainty. This was their home. And it would stay their home until her last breath. If it took marrying a stranger to keep it that way, then so be it.

Looking out the back window, Scout saw the man in question. Linc leaned against one of the fences outside of the cabins. The other five men were arrayed around him. They all listened intently as he spoke.

She could guess what that conversation was about. Their crazy idea to get married was the topic both in and out of doors. The thing was that it didn't feel crazy. It felt like the right decision.

Over the years, many people had brought their horses to Scout. They'd claimed the animals were broken, wounded beyond healing. Each time, Scout had looked into the horse's eyes and saw the truth; it wasn't the horse that was broken. Once she took the horse under her lead, the improvements were always dramatic.

Linc had that look of a wounded spirit in his dark eyes. All of the soldiers did. They all belonged here. She knew this place would heal whatever the General had put them through. In that way, the President's Men were just like her sisters. They needed a refuge to heal from his neglect and abandonment.

No, she wouldn't mind having them here at all. In fact, an even better idea would be to have her sisters each marry one of them. It didn't have to be forever. Marriage was a temporary promise if their father had taught them anything. Scout was liking this plan more and more.

"You do see that the general is meddling in our affairs from the grave," said Tilly.

The words were garbled, but Scout understood them. Scout looked up to see Tilly's mouth around a cakey mixing spoon.

"Yeah," agreed Scout. "He's still trying to get his little soldiers in formation. But this time with actual soldiers."

"I don't mind," said Brig, saddling up beside Scout to look at the men outside.

"I don't need a soldier," said Saylor. "Nick is the guy for me."

Scout didn't need to look over at Brig to see that she was sighing alongside her. All of the Silver girls agreed, even Mareen, that Nick was most definitely not the guy for Saylor. Just another reason to fall in line with the soldiers.

"How is Nick?" Brig asked, her voice pitched high with false interest. "It's been ages since we've seen him. Why don't you invite him over?"

Scout couldn't hide the wicked grin spreading across her face. From across the room, she saw Tilly's gaze narrowing in the same calculation.

"I don't think so," said Saylor. "You guys make him uncomfortable."

"Us?" said Tilly, in the same high pitch as Brig, but her tone was laced with false sincerity. "What have we done?"

"Well, there was the time you put nuts in his burger," Saylor said.

"I was trying out a new recipe."

"He's allergic to nuts."

Tilly shrugged. "It must've slipped my mind."

"Or the time you gave him Wickham to ride," Saylor turned to Scout.

Scout held up her hands in self-defense. "Hey, he said he could handle any horse."

Saylor crossed her arms over her chest and frowned at each of her sisters. "Look, guys, I know he's not your favorite person. But he's my favorite person. He's the one for me. And we all need to get married to save this place, so..."

Saylor let that sentence trail off. Scout's gaze trailed out the window. She knew how she wanted that sentence to end. But first, she had to get her own marriage underway.

"All I know," said Scout, "is that we can't afford to lose this place. It's what holds us together."

"This place isn't what holds us together," said Tilly. "Our blood holds us together."

Scout's heart pounded in her chest at Tilly's words. She loved her sisters fiercely. Though Tilly only had half their blood, Scout had never looked at the twins as anything but all hers.

"Speaking of blood," said Scout. "I'm surprised Cruella hasn't been sniffing around."

"I don't think Mareen told her," said Saylor.

"You talked to her?" asked Scout, the prickles on the backs of her hands standing straight at the thought of the bond Saylor and Mareen shared.

"She's our sister."

"Half-sister," Scout corrected.

"She's the only other sister that's getting married."

"I bet she'll call it off to spite us. Definitely, if Cruella tells her to."

Saylor didn't stand up to that remark. From what Scout knew the marriage between Mareen and Sylvester Savino was not a love match. It was more of a society match. Didn't matter to Scout as long as the two tied the knot before the end of the year.

"I still say you can't marry a stranger, Scout," Saylor was saying.

"He's not a stranger. The General vetted him."

And besides, Scout liked Lincoln Rawlings. And so did her horses. That was a good enough character reference for her.

CHAPTER TEN

"One; we can stay here indefinitely." Linc held up the first post-it and pressed it to the fencing. The yellow patch of paper stuck there. He pulled off the second note from the post-it pad. "Two; we can work with the horses. Three..."

But the post-it he held in his hand said four. Linc shuffled them around, but he couldn't find number three. What had he written down as the third reason they should each consider marrying one of the Silver sisters for the Washington Objective?

"This is just crazy." Truman threw up his hands. It was hard to miss the wince as he did so. He hunched his injured shoulder to his ear but continued his tirade. "Didn't we just leave a ranch where soldiers had to get married in order to stay there? What is this? Some cosmic craziness to force all military personnel into holy matrimony?"

"I don't know? I wouldn't mind." Jefferson fastened the sling that cradled his limp arm. They were all about to head into polite company, and he liked to keep the limb out of the way and out of sight when around others.

"You think you're ready to twirl a bride around on the dance floor," said Truman.

"Hey." Jackson pointed a blunt thumb at Truman. "That was a low blow."

Truman huffed an apology, but he did not look cowed. "It's just that I'm not a charity case."

"None of us are," said Jefferson. "What if this was apart of the general's plan all along?"

Linc still couldn't find the third reason to commence Objective Washington, but he had found the final reason he'd written down on a post-it. He held that note up for all the men to see. "We owe it to the general."

The silence in the fields was deafening. Even the animals went mute at the sight of the writing Linc posted on the fence. Their last mission for the general had been total mission failure. Though the United States Military hadn't seen it that way.

The President's Men had saved the lives of

twelve aid workers and civilians. But they'd lost their most precious asset; their leader.

"We pledged to him that we'd see that his daughters were taken care of," said Linc. "Well, this is what they need."

"But wait," said Truman. "You said he put this in his will, that his daughters had to get married to keep the ranch? And then, before he died, he made us pledge to come here."

Truman looked around the ranch. Then he looked at each man in turn. "It's a setup."

Linc shrugged. Maybe it was. Maybe this was the General's true dying wish, that his men and his daughters all become a new unit. Linc had no problem with those orders as long as he could be united with Scout.

He liked the way he felt when he was near Scout Silver. He liked gazing at her. He liked hearing her talk. Her voice rang so clearly in his head.

Linc's path was clear. Marry Scout. Make sure all of her sisters got married so they could save the ranch. Work on the ranch. Live happily ever after. He didn't even need to write that process down to remember it.

"Just have dinner with the girls," said Linc. "See if you hit it off with one of them."

"I'm keeping my mouth shut," said Truman.

"Thank God for small favors," said Jackson.

Linc turned on his heel and started for the house. As they'd done countless times before, the men all fell in line behind him. They walked into the main house, showered, and clean-shaven from the day's work on the ranch. What they saw inside the four walls of the dining room made each man groan in pure delight and hunger.

There was a veritable feast on the table. A roasted steak that was already carved sat at the center. Around the slices of meat were small potatoes whose herbaceous seasoning brought Linc closer to the table. Even the colorful salad that was off to the side of the main dish looked appetizing. There was the sweet smell of cake in the air, though unseen. Lincoln was certain the happy groans, and grumbling bellies were causing some minds to change about the mission objective he'd outlined.

"So, you're marrying my sister," said the youngest one just as Linc had lifted a healthy portion of the meal onto his plate.

What was her name again? He had it on a post-it. But he also had a knife in one hand and a fork in his other. He was not about to relinquish either to retrieve the note. So, he decided to chance it.

"Yes, Brenda-"

"It's Brig."

"Right. Sorry." Linc put down his knife. He itched to reach for the post it in his pocket, but he didn't think he could do it inconspicuously. So, he reached for the salt shaker instead.

"Not off to a good start, are you," said the blonde sister whose name Linc also couldn't remember.

Linc looked to Scout. She scowled at each sister and then turned an encouraging smile on him. Linc got lost in that smile. He forgot everyone at the table. He forgot the salt shaker in his left hand. He forgot the fork in his right.

All he saw was Scout. He wanted to impress her. He wracked his brain for the right word, the right name. And there it was. He had it.

"I'm sorry," Linc said, turning to the blonde. "I'm not so good with names. Got knocked on the head one too many times, Terry."

"It's Tilly."

Linc winced. He could feel the flush creeping up his neck and spreading across his cheeks. A bead of sweat formed on his brow. The moisture collected there, threatening to drop into his eyes. Again, his hand itched to go to the notes in his pocket.

But all eyes were on him. Instead of reaching

into his pocket, he poised the salt shaker over his steak, sprinkling the crystals over the perfectly cooked meat. When he looked up to Scout, she was frowning at him this time. He was really blowing it.

"So, Brig," said Jackson. "What is it you're studying in school? I think your father mentioned equine therapy."

"My dad talked about me?" said Brig.

"Yeah," said Jefferson. "He talked about all of you. All the time."

"He never told us anything about you," said Brig. The young woman's attention stuck on Jackson. "He never told us anything about ... anything."

"Most of it is classified," said Wilson. It was the first thing he'd said since sitting down at the table. Wilson didn't like to talk about any mission, but especially not the last one. More than any of the men, he blamed himself for the General's death.

"The General wasn't much of a talker when he was home," said Scout. "Except if it was to shout orders at us."

Linc didn't like the bitterness in her tone. He especially didn't like the hurt at the corner of her eyes. He didn't understand that. The General had loved each of his daughters fiercely. The pride in his blue eyes was clear to see each time he spoke of them.

"I'm sorry about that," said Linc. "But you should know he was very proud of each of you. He always said his daughter Scout could rehabilitate any horse you brought to her. He said Saylor could fix any broken bone on any animal. He talked about Mareen's awards in dressage. And the twins, Tilly and Gunnery, and how they'd taken the world of vaulting by storm when they were younger. And he had printouts of Brig's straight-A report cards at his desk."

Silence greeted Linc after he closed his mouth. Once again, he looked up to find all eyes on him. What had he said now? He couldn't remember. No sooner had the words left his mouth than they'd receded into the recesses of his brain.

"You got all our names right," said Brig. Her face split into a wide grin, her blue eyes shining at him.

For the first time in a long time, Linc allowed himself to grin back. He'd forgotten the pleasure of smiling at someone. He'd forgotten what it felt like to feel proud of himself.

He carved off a bite of the steak. He put it into his mouth. And he barely maintained his manners by not spitting it back out.

"Something wrong with my steak, soldier?" asked Scout.

"No, it's great." But Linc's words were choked around the salty bit of meat.

"Then why did you put a pound of salt on it?"

Linc's mind rewound back a few moments. He could remember picking up the salt shaker. And then he recalled shaking the small glass container not once, not twice, but three times.

A slight chill went through him. Again the hairs lifted on his forearms, as well as on the back of his neck. His scalp prickled with the awareness that everyone was looking at him.

"Easy now," whispered Jeff.

But Linc couldn't take it easy. He couldn't remember names. He couldn't remember handling a salt shaker. How did he think he could manage a marriage?

CHAPTER ELEVEN

Scout finished giving Bingley his morning rub down before she deposited the bale of hay in his stall. The horse let out a gust of air in thanks. Then he got to work on his breakfast.

The stalls on either side of Bingley's were empty. Both Heathcliff and Wickham were out in the corral having their breakfast with the other horses whose injuries were either healed or not pronounced enough to cause any issues. The wounded and still healing, like Bingley, remained in the barn, eating their breakfast in bed. They weren't ready for the morning meal games the others played in the corral.

Outside, three horses were snacking on three piles of hay. But after a few bites, Wickham decided he needed to try a different pile. Pinning his ears, he headed over to the next pile where Heathcliff had been happily munching. After being chased off his pile by Wickham, Heathcliff squealed at Tilney, running the gelding off to the next pile. After a few minutes of chewing, Wickham would decide he wanted some of what Heathcliff was having in the next pile, and the game of musical hay piles would start again.

The soldiers sitting around the fencing clearly found these antics amusing. Jackson slapped Wilson on the shoulder, eliciting the first grin Scout had seen from the man. Jefferson rubbed rapidly at his injured arm as he laughed alongside Carter and Truman.

Scout looked to the left and saw nothing but open pasture. She looked to the right and saw her sisters in the distance taking care of the mares' feeding in a separate pasture.

"Morning, Scout."

Scout looked up to see that Jefferson had made his way over to her. He'd captured his injured arm up in a sling.

"Morning," Scout said. "You all sleep okay?"

"Best bed I've been in in years."

"Good. Good." Scout nodded. "Breakfast should be ready soon. You all are welcome to join us."

"We appreciate that, but you know you don't have to cook for us every meal. We can take some of that work off your hands."

"Right. Sure, sure." After an awkward moment's silence, Scout cleared her throat and asked what she really wanted to know. "I haven't seen Lincoln around."

She aimed for casual, but her voice missed the mark. Whoever had just spoken sounded breathless and maybe a bit needy. Which she certainly wasn't. She was just curious.

Dinner last night had been a bust. They hadn't argued, not exactly. Could what happened even be called a disagreement?

So he hadn't liked the taste of her cooking. So he hadn't gotten the names of her sisters right the first time. Those flubs hadn't been enough to deter her. She still wanted to go forward with this marriage of convenience. The question was, did he?

"Linc went for a walk earlier to clear his head." Jeff looked off toward the western side of the property.

"Clear his head?" Each of those three words came out of her mouth with a question mark.

Jefferson sighed as he regarded her. He scratched at his chin before he spoke. "Look, you gotta give him some space from time to time. That last mission... it messed with all of us."

"Is he a danger to me?" Scout was desperate to save her ranch, but not desperate enough to put herself, her sisters, and her horses in any danger.

Jefferson's hand dropped from his chin, and his shoulders went erect, like a soldier standing at attention. "Lincoln Rawlings would never hurt you or any of your sisters. None of us would. We all pledged to your father that we would look after you. That's a promise none of us will ever break."

Scout thought over Jefferson's words. She believed him. But there was something still niggling at the back of her mind that she was missing something. "Is he a danger to himself?"

Jefferson's shoulders didn't relax into an at ease pose. They slumped in defeat. "Not in the way you think."

Jefferson pursed his lips. Indecision was clear on his face. Scout wasn't sure, but she thought she might've seen the pinky finger of his injured hand twitch.

"Despite our job, none of us are violent men. We're all still in recovery from our injuries, from the separation from the military, from trying to figure out what to do next."

"I understand," said Scout. And she did.

Though she'd never been in a war zone, her family had been through three divorces. The saying love is a battlefield was an apt one. Children of divorce have their own forms of PTSD that stay with them all their lives despite what the experts might say. And Scout would know; she'd been to her fair share of family counseling.

"Next to your father, Linc is the best man I know," said Jefferson. "I don't know why the General wrote his will the way he did. But we'd do anything to help you. We owe him that."

"So, you'll marry one of my sisters because you feel you owe our dad?"

"I'm at your service." Jeff didn't hesitate. He gave a sharp nod that felt like a salute. "It would be my honor."

His gaze lifted. Brig and Saylor were laughing as they made their way back to the house. It was good to hear Saylor laugh. She rarely did these last few years that she'd been in a relationship with The Boyfriend.

It was clear Jeff was eyeing one of her sisters. Scout just wasn't sure which one. If there could be one good thing that would come out of the General's insane will demands, it would be that The Boyfriend balked at marriage, forcing Saylor to marry one of these soldiers. Each and every one of them, even the scowling Truman would be better than Nick.

Scout grabbed a saddle from the barn and headed to the eastern pasture. Unlike the musical chairs of breakfast, Lizzie, Fanny, and Emma all ate from their own piles. No one shoved the other out of the way.

"Morning, Lizzie."

A chestnut brown head lifted from the bale of hay. The mare walked toward Scout, lowering her muzzle like a dog seeking a scratch. Scout obliged the horse, rubbing up and down the white stripe of her nose.

"Wanna go for a ride?"

Scout saddled up her horse and headed off in the direction Jeff had indicated Linc had wandered off. She passed by the old forts the Matthews and Silver kids had built when they pretended they were at war. She was happy to see that the Silver fort still looked sturdy while the Matthews structure leaned to the side.

It didn't take Scout long to find the man she was

looking for. When she spotted him, she saw that he was standing in a place she didn't want to go.

Her father's stone was right next to her mother's. They were together again finally. Though Scout wouldn't have been surprised if she'd found her father's stone turned over all these months after being laid to rest. Her parents had loved hard, but they'd fought just as hard.

Lizzie must have felt Scout's agitation because the horse let out a low whinny.

Linc looked up. His gaze caught and held onto Scout's, but he reached for the horse.

"Whoa, girl," he crooned. "Whoa, now."

Lizzie listened to Linc's gentle voice and steadied. The wobbliness Scout had felt earlier, the uncertainty of what she was doing, that also steadied at his tone. How did this man have that effect on her?

"What are you doing out here?" Scout asked.

Linc turned away from her. He looked at the horse. Then around at his surroundings. Confusion marred his strong brows for a moment. Then he looked down at the headstone. His gaze cleared as though there had never been any fog there.

"I was paying my respects," he said finally. "But I'll go if you want some time..."

"No," Scout said, dismounting.

As she swung her leg over, Linc reached up to grasp her waist. Scout placed her hands on his shoulders as he brought her to the ground.

Scout Silver was not a slight thing. She was built sturdy, like all her sisters. But Linc had just handled her as though she weighed nothing. It made her feel dainty, like something precious.

"I was just..." She let the sentence trail off. She was just what? Stalking him? "I was just coming to find you for breakfast."

"I got up early and took a walk to clear my mind," he said. "I must've gotten turned around. I didn't realize the time."

Linc looked out at the vast fields. His hold was still on her waist. Scout felt no need to move out of his embrace.

"It's easy to lose your way out here if you don't know where you're going," she said.

"Hmmm." Linc turned back to gaze down at her. "I would've found my way back eventually."

He was a foot taller than her. That was a rare thing; for a man to have much or any height on her. Both her parents had been tall; the General over six feet. Her mom just under. Scout felt small as she tilted her head back and looked up at Linc—and she liked it.

"But you found me," he continued. "When I'm around you, things are so clear."

Scout was not the type of girl that boys wrote poetry for. But that had to be the most poetic, romantic thing anyone had ever said to her. If things kept going like this with this man, she might actually have to send up thanks to her father for depositing Lincoln Rawlings on her doorstep. That would be most annoying.

"So clear, in fact, that I've come to a decision." Linc finally let her go. He took a step back, folding his hands behind his back in that way of soldiers. "I can't marry you."

Scout blinked. Then she blinked again, this time leaving her eyes narrowed on him. "You what?"

"The last mission messed me up. It messed all of us up."

"Yeah, I heard." Scout couldn't help but look over his body. Lincoln Rawlings looked like a perfectly fit specimen, except for the scar on his forehead. But even that added to his handsomeness. "You said you'd help-"

"And I will," he interrupted. "But I promised your

father that I'd do what's best for you. I believe you should marry Jackson."

Behind them, Lizzie let out a low whine. The horse backed up a few paces as though she could sense the oncoming storm.

"You're passing me off to one of your men?" said Scout.

"Jackson's a better fit for you than me," said Linc. "He's a better man than I am."

Linc ran his fingers through his hair. When he lifted his hand, a small, square piece of paper escaped his palm. The post-it sized note floated down and landed against Scout's chest.

Scout reached for the note. Flipping it over, she could barely make out the chicken scratch written there. Slowly, the squiggles and scratches began to make sense.

Reasons to let her go was written across the top. There was only one item on the list. And what she read there was unbelievable.

$\mathcal{L}$inc's first instinct had been to grab for the post-it. Though his mind was prone to fog, he knew better than to grab where the parcel of paper had landed. His mind might be muddled, but his manners were intact. So he'd kept his hands off Scout, which meant he could do nothing when she retrieved the missive from the top of her blouse.

"Please give that here," he said.

But it was too late. She'd already seen the writing on the paper. Linc had no trouble remembering those words. He'd only written the note a few minutes ago when he'd been communing with the general.

Linc had taken the time to explain to his former

commander that he wasn't fit for the mission the General had sent him on. Even though it was a job Linc desperately wanted.

Holding Scout to him a moment ago had felt like the rightest thing in the world. Letting her go so that she could stand on her own two feet, and aiming to send her in the direction of Jackson? Well, that had been the hardest thing he'd ever had to do. And he'd faced down insurgents in suicide vests.

"You don't think you're worthy of me?"

Linc closed his eyes as he heard his words come out of Scout's perfect mouth. Part of him reveled at the disbelief in her tone. His heart kicked against his chest as she narrowed her eyes in disbelief at him.

But there was still the truth in the words he'd written. And that truth stung.

"Says who?" Scout demanded. "Says him?" With the yellow post-it clutched in her palm, she pointed at her father's stone. "He barely even knew me."

That brought Linc's attention back around. "What are you talking about? He's the reason I know you."

Scout balled her fists as she glared at the gravesite. As she did so, the crinkle of the post-it note was loud in Linc's ears.

The horse walked up behind Scout. The mare nuzzled at Scout's arm. Absentmindedly, Scout reached behind and petted the horse's muzzle. Then she leaned into the mare as though seeking its comfort.

Linc wanted to be the one to wrap his arms around her. But he'd just given up that right. He wanted the best for this woman. He wished he was it, but he couldn't fool himself into being what she needed.

There were times his memories blurred. Times when he wasn't sure if he was remembering things as they were or things as he wished they were. But that hadn't been a memory. Those words were touching his ears for the first time.

"Scout, there are things you don't know about me."

"Well, there are things you don't know about me too. Like I'll do anything to save this ranch and keep my family together. My dad sent you to help, so help you will."

Now he stared at her, stunned.

"You'll marry me. Jeff is on board to marry one of my sisters. You seem to think Jackson will take the plunge, too. If Mareen keeps her wedding date, then we just have to convince one other Silver girl—

hopefully, two, if we can get rid of Saylor's boyfriend."

She turned away from the gravestone then. She looked up into Linc's eyes. He swore he could see the General staring back at him.

Linc always followed the General's command. Those actions had always come out of a sense of duty, of loyalty. What he was feeling now, looking at General Silver's eldest daughter was pure, unadulterated desire.

Linc knew then and there that the mission plan he'd drawn up, the one where he stepped aside and allowed Jackson to marry Scout would've resulted in total mission failure. Scout had the better plan. He was going to marry this woman, and he was going to do his utmost to make her happy every day of his life. No post-it note would be required for this mission.

"Okay," he surrendered.

"Okay." Her voice was terse as she handed him back the crumpled sticky note.

Linc took the scrape of paper gingerly. He shoved it into his back pocket, out of sight, and already forgotten.

"You had to write that down to tell me?" she asked.

Linc fingered the pad of unused notes in his front pocket. "Sometimes, I have trouble remembering things or keeping them in the right sequence."

Scout nodded at his admission. Just a quick bob of the head, like it didn't trouble her at all. Maybe he could do this.

"Life on a ranch is pretty monotonous," she said, her tone all business. "With daily chores and the same schedule each day, you should be fine."

Linc doubted anything would be routine with this woman, but he was willing to give it his all.

"Come on." Scout climbed up on the horse. She motioned to Linc as though he should climb on the horse's back as well.

The thought of riding with his body pressed against hers overwhelmed his senses. "I can walk back to the ranch."

"We're not going back to Silver Star just yet. We're going to see my other father."

Linc looked back at the gravesites that held both of Scout's parents. Then he looked back at her, saddled high on her horse. "Your... come again?"

CHAPTER THIRTEEN

As the midday sun rose higher in the sky, Scout wondered if she'd miscalculated. Sweat trickled down the back collar of her shirt. It was instantly cooled by the steady exhale that beat out a sure rhythm.

Linc's breath.

The man surrounded her. The hard muscles at the front of his body pressed flush up against the soft curves of her back. Though she faced forward, she smelled the earthy musk of him. It was doing things to her brain, like making her wonder what his lips would taste like. It was doing things to her body, like making her tummy grumble with want.

Lizzie trotted along under the weight of the two of them. Scout held the reins in her hands, but she was no longer certain that she was the one in control. The sound of the horse's hooves beat in time with Linc's heart. Her body swayed in time to Lizzie's clomp-clomp. But Scout still had the sense that she was falling. It was a slow descent. The fall was to the tune of a strong and sure ba-bump. Linc's heartbeats.

The reins went slack in her hands as she became lost in the sensation. It wasn't unpleasant—the falling. But it was a new experience. She'd never followed anyone else's lead but her own.

Suddenly the reins were being tugged from her hands. It was Linc. He'd taken the lead from Scout since she wasn't paying the best attention.

Scout should've demanded he give them back. But she remained mute. For the first time in her life, Scout let a man lead her. She felt safe in Linc's care, secure.

She didn't understand what he'd meant about not being the right man for her. If her body were to tell that story, it would shout that they were a perfect match.

They fit physically. They were in sync, internally. And he smelled freaking amazing.

So he was a bit forgetful. Who wasn't? She

couldn't blame a man who had spent years in combat to not want to forget some part of that life.

Besides, he was guiding her and her horse perfectly fine today. They could work on him remembering her sisters' names. They could put those post-it notes to use.

The bronze crosses of the Flying Cross Ranch came into view. The metalwork on the gate showcased the emblem with pride. The five rays of the sun extended beyond a four-bladed propeller to form a square.

"When you said your other father..." Linc started and took in a breath. "Is this...? Are we at...?"

Before Linc could find the breath or the words to complete any of those sentences, Father Matthews came to the door.

"Scout is that you? What a lovely surprise."

Linc dismounted, then he reached back to help her down from the horse. His hands on her waist felt good. So good that she momentarily forgot they had an audience.

But Linc was very aware of their audience. The softness of his body was gone. He stood erect, like a soldier greeting a superior.

"Colonel Matthews, a pleasure to meet you, sir."

"At ease soldier," Father Matthews chuckled.

It took a moment, but Linc relaxed into a slightly less stiff stance. While Linc worked to ease into the command, Scout brought herself into the colonel's embrace. Her own father had never been big on affection. Whenever Scout needed a fatherly hug, she had to go next door to receive one from her father's best friend.

"Father, I'd like you to meet Lincoln Rawlings. My fiancé."

Father Matthews's dark brows lifted up to his hairline. But he didn't look surprised.

"Yes," Scout said in answer to the older man's unasked question, "this has to do with my father's will."

Father Matthews held Scout's gaze before turning those hazel eyes onto Linc. Father Matthew's eyes always reminded Scout of sunlight. But now they looked like the sole illumination in a dark room made up for interrogation.

Linc had a few inches over the retired airman. But Father Matthews somehow looked bigger. Under the fierce scrutiny, Linc with his large muscles and sure stride, gulped like a teenager come asking a father to take his daughter to prom.

"General Silver told us many stories about you, sir."

"I'm not *sir* in these parts, son. I laid down my wings and picked up the Good Book years ago. You can call me Father Matthews."

"Yes, sir. I mean—yes, Father. I mean, Father Matthews."

Father Matthews chuckled again as he turned into the house. Scout fell in step behind him, only to find that Linc was grinning like a kid about to enter the gates of Disney Land. When Scout motioned him to join, Linc picked up his steps.

"Do you know who that is," Linc whispered as they walked into the foyer. "Colonel Matthews is a legend in the Air Force. Did you know his father was a Tuskegee Airman.? And that his great grandfather was a Buffalo Soldier?"

Scout shrugged. Sure, she knew all those things. She'd grown up hearing the stories right alongside Father Matthews's own children.

"I feel like I'm walking into U.S. Military history right now," Linc said as they came into the office.

Though Scout had been in this room countless times over her life, she always felt the same way. Linc's gaze bounced from portrait to picture to photograph on the wall. Scout's gaze lingered on the photo of the General and the Colonel standing together, grinning like they'd just gotten away with something.

"Lincoln Rawlings," said Father Matthews as he took a seat. "You're one of Abe's President's Men. He told me about you six."

Funny. The General hadn't told his daughters about the men.

The ease that had coursed through Linc's body only a moment ago appeared to seep out of him at the mention of the general. He sat at the edge of the chair before the massive oak desk. His erect back did not touch the back cushion.

"It was an honor to serve the general," said Linc.

"You're now separated?"

"Medical discharge, sir."

Father Matthews raised an eyebrow.

"I mean, Father Matthews."

"Yet somehow, I suspect you're here to continue your service to the man." Father Matthews's gaze came to rest on Scout.

Scout had years of practice being under that gaze. There were times she deserved the scrutiny, and times she didn't. In either case, she'd learned that the best thing to do was to come clean.

"We want you to marry us," said Scout.

"We do?" Linc's head whipped to Scout.

"We were thinking maybe this weekend?"

"So soon?"

Linc was all the way at the edge of his seat. One more word from her, and Scout was sure he might fall off.

"Are you changing your mind?" she asked.

"No, not at all," said Linc. "I'll do this."

"Because you owe her father?"

They both turned to look into the penetrating gaze of Father Matthews. His fingers were steepled. His mouth set in a firm line.

Linc's lips quivered. It looked as though he was about to press his teeth together to make the *yes* sound. But then he appeared to think better of that. He pressed his lips together, but when he opened them, no sound came out.

"The two of you are planning to marry to satisfy the demands of Abe's will," said Father Matthews. "I can't officiate such a pairing before the Lord."

"People around the world are forced into marriages every day," said Scout.

Father Matthews turned to Linc. "Are you being forced, son?"

"No, I want to marry her," said Linc.

Now it was Scout that was in danger of falling

out of her chair. Those words came out easily. Not a single hesitation. Not forceful. Just facts.

"I know about the will," Linc continued. "And I do feel a certain sense of responsibility for the general's daughters after..."

Now he trailed away. His gaze went over Father Matthews's shoulder. Scout knew without following Linc's eye line which picture he was looking at.

She hadn't asked exactly what had happened in that last mission. She supposed she should. Though the look of pain that darkened Linc's handsome face made her not want to go down that road.

Linc's gaze shifted and focused back on Father Matthews. "Scout's a good woman. She is efficient. Gives good direction. And she's thorough in her instructions."

"That doesn't sound like a wife," said Father Matthews. "It sounds like a job description for a member of your team."

"In the military, we become brothers for life, you know that, sir. I think those are the perfect qualities for a life partner."

Father Matthews continued to look at Linc over his steepled fingers. Finally, he pressed his palms together and laced his fingers one over the other. "Tell me, son, is this going to be one of those fake marriages where you'll get divorced after the land is secured?"

Just the sound of the D-word had Scout squirming in her seat. She had decided on this marriage. But Father Matthews was right. This family had seen enough separation. She was only doing this once, and she expected it to last forever.

"I would never leave Scout. I gave her my word. I'm not a perfect man, but I am a man of my word."

A slow grin spread across Father Matthews's face. His gaze turned from Linc and fixed on her. "All right, then. I'll marry the two of you."

Somehow his words didn't sound like a blessing. They sounded like a threat.

CHAPTER FOURTEEN

*L*inc held Scout's back to his front as they rode back to Silver Star ranch. It was solidified. They were getting married. Colonel Matthews had given his blessing, along with an interrogation worthy of a CIA operative.

They'd spent a couple of hours in the man's office as he went through a slew of pre-marital counseling questions. Colonel -Father Matthews, because with the intimate questions the man asked, he might as well be Linc's confessor. Father Matthews had asked about his financial wherewithal, his family background. He'd even delved into Linc's military background.

Linc had answered all questions, even though the beads of sweat were clearly visible all around his neck. He'd been proud that he'd answered each question, each query clearly and without a mist of fog in his brain. It wasn't until Father Matthews had asked about children that Linc had fumbled.

Children. Children with Scout. Having children with Scout. Making children with Scout.

Why hadn't that particular process crossed his mind a single time over the past day? Sure he thought about kissing her. He thought about holding her, as he was doing now. But his thoughts hadn't gone beyond that.

Now, with her back pressed to his front, they did. Linc shifted in the saddle.

"You okay back there?" she asked.

"Yeah, great."

He was not great.

As he forced his addled brain to replay all the conversations he and Scout had had about their impending nuptials, there was not one instance where they'd discussed living arrangements, specifically sleeping arrangements.

Father Matthews hadn't brought it up either. Linc supposed the old man assumed they would be sleeping together. But was that Scout's assumption?

Everything she'd said to him had been about saving her family, preserving the ranch and the animals. There hadn't been any discussion of preserving her virtue?

And then, Linc realized, it didn't matter.

Holding her to him. Standing sentry at her back. Having her trust in his guidance as he led her horse back to her home, that was enough for him.

The sun had set by the time they arrived back at the cabins surrounding the big house. He could see the lights on in the big house. The others were likely in there having dinner. Linc was hungry, but not for food. He hadn't had his fill of Scout. He wanted any morsel she was willing to give him, even if it was just more conversation.

Linc dismounted as they came to the barn. He reached up to Scout. With his hands on her waist, he was slow to bring her to standing, letting her linger in the air as she came down his body.

Scout looked up at him. He looked down at her. Her lips were there for the taking. She didn't move away.

It wasn't the most romantic setting in the world. The sounds of horses pawing the ground as they settled in for the night. The smell of manure wafting in the air.

Lizzie bumped her rump into Linc's back, sending him careening into Scout. Scout caught him in her arms, just as he wrapped her up in his embrace. They stood like that for another long moment. Until Lizzie, tired of the waiting, let out a loud whine.

Scout disentangled herself from Linc and went to put her horse up for the night. With Lizzie in bed, Linc and Scout walked side by side in silence. The direction they took was back toward the living quarters. At the fork in the road, Scout continued right, which would lead them to the cabins. The cabin he was staying in was the first cabin on the path.

Linc knew it had been built for Scout. The General had told him that he'd had his daughters each build their own home with their own hands. Which was another reason the will made no sense. Why would he have these girls build something only to take it away from them?

"We said we'd have a platonic marriage," she said.

Had they said that? Linc could not remember that conversation. One of his doctors had pondered if his memory was selective. At this moment, Linc would've given the theory credence.

"Maybe we should discuss the pros and cons of

such an arrangement," she continued. "To see if it suits us moving forward."

Linc straightened. His hand immediately itched for a post-it note to take down these new details. This was something he wanted to remember every detail of. But in his heart, he knew he would never forget the way her hair wafted in the breeze. The way her gaze was uncertain. The way her lips had a determined set to them.

Linc took the few steps to her. He wanted to kiss her, but he also didn't want to spook her with the force of his desire for her. So he held out his hand.

Scout looked at the offered appendage as though she'd never seen a man's hand before. She took it gingerly. Linc wondered if no one had ever held the woman's hand before. He gave it a reassuring squeeze and then tugged her into walking beside him.

"If I'm being honest," he began, "I never thought a platonic relationship would last between us."

Beside him, Scout stumbled. Her blue gaze went wide. Linc would've sworn he'd say the night's stars reflected in them.

"You're far too beautiful for me not to work out the process of how to kiss you."

Even in the darkness of the night, Linc could see

her blush. "You don't have to say things like that to me."

"Things like what?" he asked.

"I know I'm no stunner."

"Then you know nothing. You're the most beautiful woman I've ever seen in my life. I can't believe you're going to be mine."

Scout stopped walking. They were just a few steps from her cabin, the one he was staying in. She turned to him. The next thing he knew, his head was being yanked down, and her lips were pressed against his.

Linc forgot. He forgot everything around him. He forgot everything except for her.

She tasted of the wind, sweetened by honey. She felt like fire, cooled by a meandering breeze. Her soft, contented sigh was a wave that went over his head and pulled him under.

When she broke the kiss, she mumbled against his lips, "Invite me inside."

Linc was already walking backward with the handful that was soon to be his bride. But his steps faltered as something tugged at his consciousness. With one hand, Scout was angling to get inside the cabin she'd built with her own hands. The door was open. None of his men felt any need to lock their doors here in this idyllic setting far from any combat zone. So why was he blocking the entryway with his body?

Linc should let her in. However, there was a reason he shouldn't. But he couldn't remember it.

His side brushed against the door frame. When it did so, he felt the indent of the square pad of paper in his pocket. Every desire in him went cold.

Linc released Scout as though her skin had burned him. She wobbled on unsteady feet. He did not reach out to steady her.

"You must be hungry," he said.

"I am, but I can eat whatever you have inside."

"No, I think we should go to the house to be with the others."

Confusion was at war with the desire in her eyes. "You don't...want to?"

Linc gulped, but it was the hardest truth he'd had to swallow since the blast that had altered his life. Because he wasn't ready to recount that life-changing event, and all the consequences that came with it, Linc told Scout a different truth.

"I think we should get to know each other more," he said.

Scout took a step back. Her proud head dropped, and she stared at the ground. "Right. Of course."

Linc got the sense she was answering a question he hadn't asked. One he would never ask. "Scout..."

But she was already turning away, marching like a soldier who'd been given their orders. "I'll see you in the morning."

Linc let her go. He couldn't chase after her. Not with the burden he had behind this door.

He turned the doorknob and stepped inside. The first post-it greeted him, reminding him to lock the door behind him. There were others. They were all around the cabin with the little reminders he needed to function.

What had Linc done agreeing to marry this woman when he didn't have this under control?

CHAPTER FIFTEEN

She'd been too pushy. Scout had always been terrible with the opposite sex. With horses, she could get the animals to follow her lead. With boys or men, they often balked at her commands. Because men liked to be the ones giving the commands.

Growing up with a General for a father, she knew that lesson all too well. Still, it didn't translate in the classroom, or on the game fields, or at the local bar.

Once she opened her mouth, men would always take back their offer of a dance or a drink and turn to one of the bubbly girls in the corner. Scout didn't do bubbly. Her feet were planted too firmly on the ground.

Linc had swept her off her feet. Well, it had technically been off a horse. But she'd always climbed on and off a horse all by herself. She'd liked having a hand at the task. But then she'd pushed too hard.

Scout wasn't exactly sure what she'd done that had pushed him away. She often wasn't. But Linc had definitely turned away from her like all the other guys. Well, this fake marriage was off to a great start.

"Scoutie, pass me the eggs."

Scout pushed the carton toward Brig. Probably for the first time in her life, she didn't push hard enough. The carton teetered at the edge of the kitchen counter and smashed onto the floor.

From her place at the island, Tilly looked up from her open laptop. "What's gotten into you this morning?"

"The better question is what happened last night?" said Brig. "She and Linc were gone for hours."

"Really?" said Tilly closing her laptop.

"Yeah," said Saylor from the other end of the island where she was slicing oranges. "I don't think I heard you come in, Scout."

Scout had come inside the house last night. That was the problem. She'd come into the main house instead of into the cabin her soon-to-be-husband occupied. She'd gone alone into her bedroom. All because she'd pushed Linc too hard.

She didn't know how to be soft. At least not with humans. She had a gentle hand when it came to horses.

"We went and talked to Father Matthews," said Scout. "He said he'll marry us this weekend."

"So you're really doing this?" said Tilly.

Scout hoped she was really doing this. She hoped Linc wouldn't back out. Not just because she needed him to help fulfill the General's demands. But because she wanted him.

"I'm sorry about the eggs," Scout said, but even that came out gruff.

"It's no big deal." Brig's grin was completely unaffected. "I'll just go grab some more from the hen house. That's the beauty of living on a ranch. You have a built-in grocery store."

"No, I'll go," Scout said, already moving to the door.

Scout had to escape. Both Saylor and Tilly were slowly moving in toward her. She knew her sisters would ask a million questions about what had happened when she'd gone off with Linc yesterday. Scout didn't want to talk about it, especially the parts where she'd bumbled it. She certainly didn't want her younger sisters giving her advice about how to fix her love life. What really rubbed was that all of her sisters had more experience than she did in that arena.

Out in the circular arena of the ranch was the object of her bumbling ardor. Linc led two horses around the enclosure. Or at least he was trying to lead them.

Wickham was far more interested in trailing Anne-Elliot than following Linc's directions. For her part, Anne-Elliot was having none of either male. She pulled against her lead when Wickham fell back, trying to get a sniff of her.

Scout picked up her steps as she hurried inside the gate. Linc was managing the situation. The man worked well with the horses. The man simply worked well.

Scout loved seeing the powerful build of him. The strength in his hands. The problem was he had no idea what he was in the middle of with the two horses.

In fact, he didn't appear to notice any issue between the horses at all. Linc looked off in the distance. His gaze clouded over. He even slowed his pace, grinding both horses to a halt. That was all Wickham needed.

The horse broke free of Linc's hold. Wickham fell back, aiming to get around the inattentive human and at the buxom beauty on the other side. That's when Anne-Elliot broke free of Linc's hold as well. She trotted off, evading Wickham's attentions.

Scout took a step back toward the fence as the horses passed her. When she turned to find Linc, what she found were strong arms coming around her.

"Scout," Linc said, his hands running up and down her arms. "Are you hurt?"

"No, I'm fine."

She was more than fine. She was back in his arms. And Scout wasn't entirely sure her feet were on the ground.

"I don't know what happened?" said Linc, his gaze still hazy.

"We're having a baby."

He blinked, his eyes filling with clear alertness. "A baby?"

"Anne-Elliot, she's pregnant."

"Anne-Elliot?"

"The mare."

Linc looked over at the two horses. Wickham was walking with his head hung low after being rejected by the pregnant mare.

"You have to be careful with a pregnant mare, especially around males."

"I thought she was male," said Linc, his brows pinched in confusion.

"No, if you look hard enough, it's pretty obvious she's a girl."

Now Linc's lips pursed to match his brows. "I must not have been thinking clearly."

Linc rubbed at his head. Before Scout knew it, her hand was on his temple. It was a pushy move. But she couldn't find it in herself to regret the touch or pull her hand away.

Looked like she wouldn't need to. Linc turned his face into her palm. He nuzzled it as would one of her horses who wanted to be stroked.

Scout's fingers tingled as she touched him. Linc gave himself, well his head, completely over to her. She felt the same trust coming from him that she had with her horses.

"Hmmm," he sighed.

Or was that a groan? She wasn't good at reading the sounds of men.

"Is your head bothering you?" she asked.

Linc stepped closer to her. His strong chest came flush against hers. If he did answer, Scout couldn't hear him over the beat of her heart.

His hand rested on her hip. A moment later, he pulled her closer. "Everything feels so clear when I'm with you."

Linc's forehead came to rest against hers. Scout knew she should hold back. She should wait for him to make his move. But she'd never been good at standing by. She lifted her head and captured his lower lip.

Linc inhaled. Or was that a gasp? Just another male sound she wasn't sure how to categorize. When Linc's top lip took hold of hers, Scout decided it was a good sound.

He pulled her even closer, deepening the kiss. But as he did so, there was an unsteadiness to the hold. They broke the kiss, still clinging to one another. Scout wasn't sure who was holding whom up. She certainly felt dizzy. But there was a pained expression on Linc's face.

"Hey," she said.

He opened his eyes. His gaze was once more

cloudy. It took him a minute to focus on her. "I'm sorry. I forgot myself there."

He stepped back, letting her go. But his steps were unsure, and he reached for the railing.

"Do you need an aspirin? There's some in your cabin in the first aid kit. I'll go grab it for you."

Linc's eyes flashed wide. Any trace of fog blew out the way. "No, I'm fine."

Scout swallowed. It was a hard maneuver with all the desire still stuck in her throat.

"I'm sorry," he said.

Scout didn't dare ask what he was sorry for. If he said he was sorry for that kiss they'd just shared, she would die of mortification. "I should put Anne-Elliot out to pasture with the other mares."

"What about the babies," he said, but then frowned. He pinched the bridge at his nose. "No, I mean eggs. You said you needed eggs, right?"

Scout nodded. She'd forgotten about the eggs.

"I can get those for you," he said.

"Thank you." The words sounded lame to her ears. She'd just been wrapped up in this man's embrace, pressing her body against his.

Linc nodded. He stuck his hand in his pocket and turned on his heel. As Scout watched him hesitate at the gate, he pulled out a square pad. He quickly jotted something down and then pushed out the gate.

It was likely another reason to let her go. All because she had pushed him again. When would she ever learn?

CHAPTER SIXTEEN

Linc stood in the middle of the hen house. He looked around. He couldn't remember what he was doing here. All he could remember was the feel of Scout's fingers rubbing against his temples. The soothing scent of her breath hitting his skin. The oblivion that took him when he claimed her mouth for his own.

Babies. She'd spoken of babies. That thought stuck in his head.

Could he be a father? What if he messed up a simple process like changing a diaper? What if one day he forgot some important detail about his child?

But that was his fear talking. His heart was beating loudly in his ears. His heart wanted to make a baby with Scout. His heart wanted to make a life with Scout.

She was his new mission in life, his sole purpose. That thought, he could keep straight. But no other sequence seemed to stick.

He looked down at his post-it note. His writing looked like chicken scratch. Soon he was able to decipher his hurried scrawl. *Get Scout babies.*

That could not be right. But he had flashes of memories of her saying something to him about babies. The horse, the mare, she was pregnant. Walking to them together had been a mistake he should've caught. If he'd just looked closely, he would've noticed the difference in the two horses he'd brought into the pen.

Linc was trying to develop a routine at the Silver Star Ranch. He thrived in monotony. But each day brought a new and exciting adventure with Scout.

He was having a hard time finding his way. What he needed to do was to sit down with Scout and tell her everything. Everything about that last mission. Everything about his injury. He'd have to eventually. They were going to be married soon. She would know. Especially if they were going to be married in the true way and share living space.

And man did Linc want to be married in the

truest of ways. But he didn't want to share the extent of his condition with her. Not the memory fog. Not the confusion. Not the frustration of forgetting the simplest tasks, the request just made of him a moment ago that slipped through the cracks of his fractured brain.

Scout looked at him like he was a whole man. She looked at all the men as though they were abled bodies and not broken men. She treated her horses the same way, expecting them to perform - not regardless of their injuries- but in spite of them.

If any woman would understand what he was going through, maybe it would be her?

Back in the hen house, the rooster strutted his stuff amongst the hens. That had been Linc in the past. He'd had his choice of women. Had he looked that ridiculous? He couldn't remember, and that was likely for the best.

All he wanted to do now was to be the best man he could be for the woman he was going to spend the rest of his life with. Her father had seen excellence in him. But that excellence had fallen short when the general had needed it most. When The President's Men should have been protecting the General with their lives, it had been General

Silver who had made the ultimate sacrifice to protect his men.

Linc tried not to dwell on that. He knew he couldn't change the past. That was something he tried to stress to his men. Wilson still had trouble with it. Because Wilson had been the closest to the General when it had happened.

"Oh, hey, good morning, Linc."

Linc turned to see the youngest Silver Sister. He wanted to reach into his pocket for the post-it he'd prepared on the sisters, but the chart he'd created flashed in his mind. Each of the Silver girls was named after a military rank or object.

"Good morning, Brigadear."

She gave him a nod, her features filled with what looked like respect. "You know I always wanted a brother. And now I'm getting six. Well, five if I can bag one of you for my own husband."

Linc may have been able to recall the girl's name, but he was having trouble following the line of conversation. Brig talked so fast and switched topics so fluidly that he was having trouble keeping pace. She might favor her older sister, but the younger version of Scout didn't help keep Linc's train of thought clear and in focus.

"I came to get some eggs for breakfast since

Scout dropped the ones from earlier. But she didn't come back. Wait, is she in here with you? Were you guys making out?"

All Linc caught from that was Scout and eggs. She'd said something about babies and eggs. He put those two together and remembered why he was in here. He said he'd get the eggs for her. But he'd forgotten. Even his note to himself hadn't been clear.

Likely because his mind had been preoccupied with other thoughts.

"So tell me, did my dad, like, assign one of you guys for each of us?"

"What?" Linc turned his attention back to Brig.

"Because I think he did. And I think he got it right with you and Scout. You're perfect for each other."

"We are?"

"It's clear Saylor and Jeff would make a perfect match, too. But she's still stuck on that awful boyfriend of hers. We've been trying to break them up for years. Dad couldn't stand him either."

"Brig, can we go back to what you said about me and Scout-"

"I'm not sure who he would've picked for me? Who do you think? Wilson seems too severe. I bet he'd get along with Mareen. Too bad she's already getting married. Probably Carter? But I've seen him eyeing Tilly. That leaves Truman and Jackson. Exactly how old is Jackson?"

Linc had long since lost the thread of the conversation. The only thing he clung to was that the General thought he was the man for the job when it came to his eldest daughter. Linc might've messed up with the eggs and the horses. But maybe he could pull this mission—this marriage—off.

CHAPTER SEVENTEEN

Scout had to continually slow her steps as she led Anne-Elliott out to pasture. The broodmare was twenty-one years old, far past the age that a horse should be carrying. But her former owner had been a greedy, uncaring woman. She'd only looked at the horse as a cash cow, or rather cash horse. After the last pregnancy, the Animal Welfare League had stepped in. But it had been too late to prevent this pregnancy.

They'd brought Anne-Elliott to the Silver Star Ranch when they realized the mare was with her twelfth calf. It was going to be a rocky birth, but the horse had the two best women for the job. Scout and Saylor would help the old gal through the birth every step of the way. And the best part was that the former owner would see no profit from it.

Horses Scout didn't have to push. They naturally went where she wanted them to. Even the stubborn ones eventually caved to her demands. Why couldn't human males be the same?

Looking ahead, Scout saw a man in the pasture with the other mares. He had the same upright posture of all the soldiers. The only reason she could tell him from the others was by the way he held his arm.

Jefferson worked to roll out a bale of hay, one-handed. Her horses waited patiently for the man to perform the task. Once their breakfast was in place, the ladies gathered around. These mares weren't prone to shoving each other aside like some of her males in the other pasture.

Jefferson reached up and patted at Lizzie's muzzle. When he did so, Scout noticed the scrape on his limp arm. Blood trickled down from his elbow, likely a wound from the rough ties on the rope.

"Jefferson," she called out.

He lifted his head with a welcoming smile as she came into the gate. There was a sense of pride in the man's eyes. It was a look Scout knew well. It was the look her horses gave her when they accomplished a task she'd set them to.

Jefferson was out here on his own. She knew these men had all been separated from the military due to their injuries. She figured most of them weren't sure what to do with themselves if not on a mission. Scout was happy to allow them to find a new purpose on this ranch.

"Morning, Ms. Silver."

"Please, call me Scout. It looks like you've got yourself a minor wound there."

Jefferson pursed his lips as he looked down at his left arm. The look in his eyes said he wanted to brush it off as nothing. If he did, Scout would have to resort to her pushy ways.

It wasn't a minor wound. The blood continued to run freely. They had to get it bandaged soon.

"I should've put the sling on," Jeff said, sounding entirely reasonable. "You got a first aid kit nearby?"

"Yeah, come with me."

The closest place was the cabin where Linc was staying. She guided Jefferson the short distance there while he used the edge of his shirt to stave off much of the blood. When he looked up to see where they'd arrived, he got that pinched look on his face again.

"There's a first aid kit in my cabin," said Scout.

"No, wait," said Jefferson. He lifted his free hand to her but pulled it back before his bloodied fingers could touch her.

"Don't worry, Linc isn't in here. He's in the chicken coop gathering eggs for breakfast."

The door was unlocked, as always. It was dark inside, but she didn't need the light. She knew this cabin like the back of her hand. She'd helped build it. She'd helped build them all as the eldest. Hers had taken the longest since it had only been her and her dad when they'd started.

But Scout didn't like to think of those times. In the echo chamber in her mind, she could've sworn she heard a rumbling sound in those memories. Sometimes, she thought the sound was laughter. But that wasn't possible. It was just her and her dad.

Scout made her way past the sparse furniture until she was in the bathroom. She flicked the light on then and froze. There were post-it notes on the mirror above the sink.

Objective; Personal Grooming, was written in bold block letters. Beneath in a slimmer marker was written a list of tasks; *shave daily, brush teeth, floss,* and a few others.

She already recognized Linc's handwriting from the first post-it she'd seen of his. Scout touched the note. It felt intimate to see the inner workings of his mind.

Feeling as though she were intruding on his personal thoughts, she grabbed the first aid kit and turned. Before she turned out the light, something across the hall in the bedroom caught her attention.

The sheets on the four-poster bed were done with military precision, the way all the Silver girls had been taught in their youth. There were no clothes on the floor, nothing out of place. But that's not what caught her attention.

There was another array of post-its on the wall. This time *Night Routine* was written in bold as the Objective. Beneath the objective was a set of new tasks related to sleep preparation. Things like *make a to-do list for tomorrow, consult today's to-do list, mental exercises, check locks, and home security.*

Linc had said he had trouble remembering things. But he's said more. He'd said he had trouble keeping things in the right sequence. Is this how he was coping with that issue?

Stepping back into the hall, Scout flipped the

light switch on for the main room. Post-it notes were on the small fridge about meal prepping and eating times

On the wall closest to the door was the most extensive array of post-its. The coordinated colors were a thing of beauty. But it was the mission objectives that set Scout back on her heel.

Primary Mission; Save Silver Star Ranch.

There was an array of tasks listed below. Things like *Assign men jobs. Improve working of the ranch.* And then, *select potential wives.*

Scout saw each of her sisters' names, filled with a few words about their personalities. Beneath those were the names of the soldiers and their listed character strengths. String dangled from the post-its, but only one string was attached.

Scout's pink post-it was attached to Linc's blue post-it.

It might have been romantic, but for the cold, calculating words surrounding the connection.

Acquire Scout's hand in marriage. Along with a *Task Complete* scrawled on the bottom. But that was not the end.

Beneath that was a new post-it. The first read *Deliverable; marriage.* Written beneath that was the date they'd agreed to have the ceremony.

"Scout..."

Scout whirled around to face Jeff, nearly dropping the collection of bandages she'd gathered from the bathroom. She'd forgotten he was here. He held his arm. Red seeped between his fingers. Right, that's why she was holding the First Aid Kit in her hand.

"You have to understand..." Jefferson was saying. "He's had a traumatic brain injury. We all have. It's affected us in different ways."

"He said he had trouble keeping things in order," Scout said as she turned away from the mission board.

"He has trouble sequencing events. It helps him to map out processes."

Scout nodded instead of speaking. Her head whirled. The words *mission* and *objective* and *tasks* kept playing in her head. Those were words her father always used.

The General was always away on a mission. He couldn't return until he'd met his objective. He'd always give the girls tasks to complete.

"It may sound clinical," said Jeff, "but it's how his brain works best."

"No, I get it. I'm a mission to complete."

Jeff winced. "That's not—"

"What are you doing in here?"

Both Scout and Jeff looked up to see Lincoln darkening the doorway. His eyes clear as he took the two of them in. His face was set in a grimace of anger.

CHAPTER EIGHTEEN

Linc had gone on high alert when he saw the door to his cabin open. His mind instantly cleared and told him that there had been a breach. His typical protocol would have been to lock the door. But after a couple of days on the ranch, he had come to know there were no enemies present. He'd felt safe and secure here. He was surrounded by his men.

But the open door was not something his men would do. They had had so little privacy in the service that they wouldn't dare intrude on another man's space. So it couldn't be one of his men.

That left one of the girls. This was their home, not his. They had every right to go in and out of the cabins.

But that wasn't the issue. If someone was inside, they were seeing things he didn't want to be shown. His post-its were on display. It was as though the entire contents of his mind were laid out in the open, making him vulnerable. His worst fears were realized when he heard the sultry voice from inside.

Scout was hunched over Jefferson. Jealousy, white and hot, briefly shoved aside Linc's shame at her nearness to Jeff. She was bent over him, too close for Linc's comfort. Then he saw the bandage in Scout's hand and the blood on Jeff's arm.

"I had a disagreement with a bale of hay," said Jeff, using his free hand to hold up his bleeding arm so that Linc could see."

But Linc had already come to that conclusion and moved past. His attention was focused on Scout, whose attention was focused on the process map on the wall of the main room. Lincoln felt lobotomized with both Scout's and Jeff's gaze on the array.

"I'll let you two talk," said Jeff. Before he went out the door, he laid a hand on Linc's shoulder. Linc's second in command gave him a meaningful look, one that said take it easy.

Lincoln took a deep breath, preparing to do just that. He'd already resolved to tell Scout about the extent of his brain injury. Looked like it was time to both tell as well as show.

"Task complete, huh?" said Scout, her gaze trained on the post-its on the wall.

Scout's voice sounded different to him. There was still the bossy edge that Linc liked. But he also heard a hint of hurt in her voice. Had she been hurt alongside Jeff? He hadn't even considered that.

Linc was in front of her in two strides. He looked her over. But all of her skin was intact. Nothing appeared out of order. She looked whole, but something told him that there was still something wrong. Maybe something internal?

"What is it?" he asked. "Are you hurt?"

Scout's eyes flashed to his. "Am I hurt? How can you ask me that?"

Scout had always made Linc's mind clear, but now things went hazy. She looked angry, and he couldn't understand why? She looked like she was in pain, but there were no open wounds.

"Tell me the truth," she said, finally turning her gaze away from the papers on the wall and onto him. "Did the general assign you to me?"

The General? Assignments? This harkened back to the conversation Linc had just had with Brig about their commander assigning a man to each of his daughters.

"No, General Silver didn't assign us to you. Like I said, he asked us to come and check on you in the case of his untimely death. That's why we're here."

"So you made me your objective?"

Yes, she was his objective. Securing Scout's hand, her happiness, that was Linc's new life mission. But how did he say that to her without sounding like a crazy person? It was too soon to feel what he was feeling.

"I don't know whether to be afraid of you or not," Scout said, confirming his fears. "This wall is what a serial killer would have in his place."

Linc tore his gaze away from her and looked at the wall. The wall looked the way they would organize most of their missions. Tasks, objectives, deliverables. He could see how it could be a little disconcerting when hers and her sisters' names were part of the mission.

"This was how your father always outlined our missions. Down to the last one. And just like now, that mission didn't go as expected."

Scout's shoulder's tensed at the mention of her father. He knew what the girls had been told, that their father had been killed in the line of duty.

Families weren't often given the exact details as most of the unit's missions were classified.

Linc pinched the bridge of his nose as scenes from that fateful day flashed behind his closed eyes. His mind threatened to fog, but he had to stay clear on this. It was mission critical.

"We were sent to rescue an American diplomat and his family; a father and his two children who were trapped in an embassy. We made it in but got pinned down as the facility came under heavy fire."

Linc opened his eyes, but his gaze remained lowered. He felt if he lifted his head any higher, he would meet the sun's glare from the window, and the memories would burn away. He didn't want that. He owed it to the general to remember the truth of that day.

"They call us heroes, but we failed that mission. We lost a prized asset; your father."

The unit had completed each task. The objectives had been met. The mission had succeeded, even though the outcome had not been what they'd expected.

Linc had always trusted the general's planning. He'd never questioned the man's logic or motives. Not even when they'd failed them on that fateful day.

"I don't want to be your mission," Scout said, her voice sounding choked.

At the sound of those words, Linc's mind didn't fog. The world inside Linc began to darken. "You don't want to marry me?"

"I..." Scout's chin wobbled. And then... tears.

Lincoln was at a loss on what to do. He didn't have a process map for calming a crying woman. He held out his hands, but did she want to be held? Her hands were fluttering in front of her, sending a ripple through the post-its on the wall.

"Scout, I know I'm not a whole man with this..." Linc motioned to his head. There was no fog there now. His objective was clear. "But I swear I'll work my hardest to complete these tasks and make this mission a success. Failure is not an option."

Linc hoped those were the right words. He hoped that she would fling herself into his arms. He hoped they would end this debacle in a breathless kiss.

Instead, she let out an agonized cry and stormed out the front door, slamming it behind her. With the harsh wind from the door, some of his post-it notes fell from the wall.

CHAPTER NINETEEN

Scout paced the length of the barn.

Luckily it was empty. Otherwise, the way her boots ate up the ground would've agitated the horses.

She didn't want to return to the house and face her sisters with her failure. She couldn't return to the cabin where the evidence was written on the walls. She'd been right all along.

They were nothing but a mission. The plan was written in colorful sticky notes on Linc's wall. She was an order for him to follow. An objective for him to accomplish. A task for him to execute.

She had to give it to him. It was a good plan. One she could've plotted herself. One she'd tried to plot herself in getting all of her sisters married so that she could save the ranch. What she couldn't abide was her father's hand in this mess.

Because it had his handiwork written all over it. Though it was Linc's handwriting on the walls. But he was just following orders.

He couldn't have any real feelings for her. Right?

"Can you feel that?"

The voice came from the other side of the barn walls. It was Saylor. It was her doctor's voice.

As a veterinarian, Saylor often talked to the animals in her care as though they could understand her. Scout knew that most of them could. Even more that sometimes they responded.

"Can't feel a thing," came a deep male voice.

Scout started. She knew that voice. She'd just left that voice.

"Well, I've got you bandaged up now," said Saylor.

Scout winced at that. She had been tasked with bandaging up Jefferson. But she'd been derelict on those duties once she saw the post-its.

"Thank you, Saylor."

"So, hey, tell me the truth. Did the General give you orders to marry us?"

"No. He told us about each of you. But before

he... he made us pledge to come here and look after you all."

"Look after us?"

"Matrimony wasn't the mission, but if that's what you need..."

Scout chanced a glance around the corner in the ensuing silence. She might be upset about what she'd just seen on Linc's walls, but she'd put all her pride aside if a good man like Jefferson caught her sister's eye.

Saylor clearly didn't notice the interest in Jeff's voice. She wasn't even looking into his eyes, which were fixed on her. She was still checking out his wound.

A ringing phone cut through the silence. "That's my boyfriend. I'll need to get it. I've been waiting for his call since yesterday."

The disappointment that clouded Jeff's face at Saylor's departure mirrored Scout's. They both watched Saylor walk off to take the call. Scout wished her sister could see the man behind her who'd cared enough to offer his hand just a few days after knowing her to ensure her livelihood and wellbeing. Instead, Saylor was off kowtowing to a creep who barely acknowledged her existence.

But then again, who was she to talk. Scout had

just stormed off from a man who had diagramed how to give her and her sisters what she needed.

She couldn't figure out what upset her most? The fact that Linc had his own plans to give her what she wanted? Or that he didn't have any actual feelings for her? She was only a mission objective he'd been tasked with.

Linc didn't care for her. He never could. Just like her father. At the end of the day, it was always about the mission.

"I don't suppose it went well back there?"

Scout looked up to see Jefferson approach, his one arm outstretched. The other arm at his side. The bandage in place.

"You think?" said Scout.

"Well, with the steam coming out of your ears, and the way you're pawing at the ground, I'd say you're ready to charge."

"Wouldn't you be if you realized the man you..." Scout swallowed. She couldn't believe she was about to admit that she was falling for Linc. But the truth was she had fallen for him.

"I know Linc's methods might be confusing-"

"You mean the serial killer wall of post-its?"

Jeff winced. "He's a meticulous man. He was always very detail-oriented. But he can't keep all the details straight in his head anymore. He writes them down, so he has a visual representation. That's how he organizes the things that are most important to him."

That called Scout up short. She kicked at the ground, but the rock was embedded in the earth, and she stubbed her toe. The things that are most important to him? She had been a fixture on Linc's wall. Did that mean that she was important to him?

"But he called me a mission? He put our marriage down as an objective. I was just a task on his list."

"Scout, that's just how soldiers speak," said Jeff. "He made you his mission, but you're missing the point. He made you his end game. Do you know what an end game is?"

Scout had heard her father talk about an elusive final mission. The last one he'd take, the one that would bring him home... someday. But someday had never happened.

"An end game is a final mission. Linc wants you to be his final mission, and he plotted out the best way to make that happen."

CHAPTER TWENTY

Linc stayed inside, completely immobile after Scout had stormed off. For long moments, he simply stared at the wall of post-its. Though there was a clear plan of action outlined for him, he didn't know what to do next.

Should he go find her? Should he give her time? There was no game plan for that line of action. What he did know was that he could not stand still for the rest of the day. He was a man of action, and so he stepped outside.

The bright light of the sun hurt Linc's eyes when he stepped out of the cabin. He let the rays burn into his brain, hoping they would make his next action clear. But it was as though he walked through a cloud of steam.

His traumatic brain injury had robbed him of his dream to serve longer in the military. Just as soon as he was coming to accept his new fate, a life on this ranch with Scout in his arms, it looked that that would blow up in his face.

Maybe he'd been delusional to think that such a strong woman would take on a wounded man like him. He could no longer lead his men. Did he really think he could be the man she needed both in her work as well as in her heart?

By the way she'd walked off, he knew the answer was clearly no. But that was the only clarity he had. He didn't know what to do with himself now.

In the distance, he saw Wickham running around the pasture. The horse was making mischief this morning. He ran off Bingley, who was nibbling at a bale of hay. But no sooner had the blond horse moved onto a new bale did Wickham run him off again.

Linc made his way to the pasture. As he did so, he caught the dark horse's gaze. Wickham sauntered up to the gate and put his head over the fencing as though seeking a pat on the head. Clearly, the horse needed some extra attention. That Linc could handle.

Taking the horse by its lead, Linc walked into the

barn. Wickham gave a tug of the reins. Linc held his ground, waiting until the horse settled down. Once Wickham calmed, Linc managed to fit the horse with a riding saddle. When the horse continued to behave, Linc mounted him.

Atop the horse, power surged through Linc's body. There was nothing like riding a horse to make a man feel in control. The horses at the Purple Heart Ranch had all been docile, gentle creatures. Wickham needed a strong hand. Though Linc's mind sometimes blurred, he still had strength in his hands.

Linc gave a gentle tug of the reins to get the horse's attention. Then giving a squeeze with his thighs, he urged the horse to walk on. Wickham obeyed without a single hesitation. Clearly, the horse needed to get the exercise as much as Linc wanted to give it.

The other horses lifted their heads as the two of them walked by. Once they were clear of the pastures where the mares were being fed, Linc found the trail he'd rode with Scout. He put Wickham on that path and let the horse pick up speed.

With the sun on his back and a little wind in his

hair, the fog in Linc's mind began to dissipate. Scout's face was all he could see in his mind's eye.

He'd drawn out a process to win her. He'd almost accomplished that mission. But then she'd seen his process and walked away.

All Linc could think about was Scout's reaction to his post-its. If they were the problem, then he'd get rid of them. What he couldn't change was his end game.

Those pathways he'd strung with paper and string were, in reality, set in stone. Or rather in vessels and veins. Because Scout Silver was now in Linc's heart.

He loved her bossy attitude. She thought she was pushy? She had nothing on him when he set his mind to something. No matter which way he turned, no matter what direction he looked, he knew that from this moment onward it would always lead back to her.

Except, looking around, Linc wasn't sure where he was. They were no longer on any discernible path. He'd been so lost in his head that Wickham had led them astray.

He looked up to the sun to get his bearings, but the sky was cloudy. The sun hid hits locations.

He couldn't see the ranch house or the cabins.

The skyline was uniform. All around him, everything looked the same. He might go one direction only to end up even further from his goal, which was to get back to Scout.

He hadn't bothered bringing his cell phone as service was spotty out here. So he couldn't call for help. He had a pad of post-its in his pocket, but all the square sheets were blank.

Linc didn't need to put pen to paper. He knew where he wanted to go. He'd simply have to pick his way back there. He'd muddle through the green monotony of the land until he was back to Scout. It might not be a straight shot. The process might not be pretty. But he knew whatever move he made would lead him back to her.

He gave a tug of the reins. Instead of heeding his command, Linc felt Wickham beginning to rear. His immediate reaction was to pull the horse tighter to assert his control. But as seemed the theme of the day, Linc had to admit he wasn't the one in control at this moment. And so he loosened the reins.

Dismounting was not an option. Linc aimed to stay centered in his saddle. He leaned forward, tipping his body toward Wickham's neck and waiting until the horse's feet were back on solid ground.

With Wickham's feet on the ground and Linc's hands still on the reins, Linc continued to lean forward. He kept his breathing and his emotions calm. There was no need to yell. The horse had tried him, as an alpha horse might be want to do. But Linc had kept his head. Now that the horse realized Linc couldn't be led, he walked on as though nothing had happened.

But for Linc, everything had changed. This little tug of war had shown him that his instincts never led him astray. That even in a fugue state where he was lost and unsure of his surroundings, he could always trust his gut, his intuition.

Now, if only his gut could point him in the right direction back to the woman he loved.

"Lost your way, son?"

Lincoln looked over to see a larger than life Black man on an Arabian. Father Matthews wore a dark cowboy hat, but there were no shadows cast on his serene face. His hazel eyes twinkled as he regarded Linc.

"Not at all, Father. I'm on my way back to her." Linc urged Wickham to turn right. Then left. He looked back up to Father Mathews. "But if you could point me in the right direction so I can get there faster?"

CHAPTER TWENTY-ONE

The last time anyone had seen Linc had been when he'd come out of the barn. Jackson had said he'd seen the man mounted atop Wickham. Scout's heart stopped. Wickham hadn't let a soul mount him since he'd come here.

Perhaps Jackson was wrong about which horse Linc had ridden out on. But no. Wickham's stall was empty. There was a saddle missing from the tack wall Linc and his men had organized the other day.

"Which way did he go?" Scout demanded.

She followed the direction of Jackson's finger. It was toward the Flying Cross Ranch. The path between the two ranches was well-tread. If Linc had ridden off on any other horse, Scout wouldn't worry. But that it was Wickham made her concerned.

"I'll round up the guys," said Jackson.

"No, I'll get there faster on my own."

"But you're not on your own, Scout. We were your father's unit. Now that you're with Linc, we're your family."

The corners of Scout's eyes pricked with tears. She didn't have time to let them fall. "I pushed him away. I've gotta bring him back."

As though Lizzie knew she was needed to save the day, she trotted over to Scout as Scout came into the pasture with her saddle in hand. Once situated, Lizzie raced down the path the two of them had taken for years. If Wickham had misbehaved as Scout expected him to, then the horse and Linc wouldn't have gotten far. But she and Lizzie were pretty far along the path, and they hadn't come across the two.

Maybe there was nothing to fear after all? Wickham had taken to Linc. Perhaps the two were getting along just fine?

Even if that were true, Scout needed to find Linc. It was her mission. She didn't want there to be any more distance or misunderstandings between them. He was her end game. Whether it be her father's will or not.

And speak of the devil. The sight of her father's headstone caught Scout's eyes. Without even realizing she was doing it, she slowed Lizzie and urged her to the clearing of the family gravesite.

Her sense of urgency for Linc momentarily waylaid, Scout climbed down off her horse. With a pat, she allowed Lizzie to go and graze on the bright flowers poking up from the ground. Her mother had planted the horse-friendly flowers before she'd been laid to rest. Sarah Silver had wanted the beloved animals to visit her in death.

Scout ran her fingers over her mother's gravestone. Off to the side of her mother's final resting place sat another tombstone. It read *Roxanne Silver, loving wife, devoted mother until the day she died.*

Roxanne had been the General's third wife. Well, technically, his fourth since her parents had married and divorced again briefly. Scout had been determined to dislike the woman as much as she'd disliked Catherine the Cruel. But Roxanne had been diagnosed with cancer shortly after the twins were born, and everything changed. During those dark days, Scout had overheard the conversation between her mom and her second stepmom that had changed her and her sisters' lives.

"You're not on your own," Sarah had said to Roxanne. "Our girls are family." And then, after a deep breath and with a lift of her chin, Sarah said three words that were rarely heard between two women who'd married the same man. "We're your family."

The words echoed what Jackson had just said to her. Scout's gaze swung to her father's stone. As per his wishes, there was no inscription on his stone save for the hard cold facts of his birth date and the day of his death.

How had this man brought together so many people while being apart from them at the same time? He was always ready to give an order. But Scout never knew what he was thinking. She never understood why he did what he did.

"You were a great leader," Scout said to the earth that cradled her father. "I just wish you'd let me in, that you'd talked to me more. Then maybe I wouldn't question your judgment so much."

The stone stared silently at her.

"If you did send him to me, if you made me Linc's mission—"

"He didn't."

Scout didn't turn to the sound of the deep voice

coming from behind her. Her gaze stayed focused on her father's gravestone.

"I made you my mission," Linc continued. "You will always be my mission, even if I have to fight for you for the rest of my days."

Scout turned in time to see Linc dismount from Wickham. The horse turned its head to rub its muzzle against Linc's arm, as though nudging the man forward. Scout caught a glimpse of Father Matthews before he tipped his hat and walked off on his Arabian.

"I'll see you two this weekend," the older man muttered with a smile. "At your wedding ceremony."

Scout couldn't take her eyes off Linc as he marched toward her. He looked every bit the soldier striding forth to claim his victory. His purposeful strides were taking far too long for her, so she raced to him and leaped into his arms.

"I thought I lost you," she said into his neck as he wrapped her uptight.

"I was headed back to you. I just lost my way for a moment."

"I'll draw you a map. We can put it on a post-it, so it fits in your pocket."

Scout pressed her body into his, needing to get

closer to this man. Linc might not always see the path clearly, but he had no problem in letting her take the lead in a process. Which was precisely why she would never have any trouble following behind him.

"About the mission wall," he said, pulling away from her. "I'll take it down if it upsets you."

"Don't," she said, running her fingers through his thick hair like she'd wanted to do since the moment she met him. "It freaked me out at first. But now that I'm seeing clearly, that wall, your process, it helped me to understand you better. It let me know what you're thinking."

"All I think about is you. How to win you. How to be the man you need."

"You are exactly what I need," she said. "And you've done it."

"Done what?"

"You've won me. I'm yours."

"What you're saying is mission accomplished?"

"Roger that."

"Permission to engage with friendly fire?"

"Permission granted."

Linc pressed his mouth to hers. With the first touch, Scout felt a spark light in her heart. With the second brush of his lips, she felt her soul ignite.

All the while, her soldier was there. Keeping her safe and secure. Making her feel wanted and adored. Letting her know that he would never lead her into harm's way. That with his kiss he pledged to honor her every day for the rest of their lives.

CHAPTER TWENTY-TWO

*L*inc pulled the last sticky note from the bathroom mirror. The adhesive gave without protest. It made a crackling sound as he crinkled it up in the palm of his hand. With a flick of his wrist, the wadded missive landed in the wastebasket with the others.

With the note gone, Linc got a clear view of his face. He was cleanly shaven. His hair trimmed. Stepping back to get more of a view, he could admit that he looked handsome in the suit he'd picked up from in town.

The town's folk had eyed him skeptically as he and his men did their shopping the other day. The six strangers had only been in town a week, and yet here they were shopping for wedding clothes.

Outside of following them with their eyes, no one made a peep.

Outside the cabin, some of those same people were gathered. They awaited the main event. The wedding of Scout Silver and one of her father's soldiers.

A knock sounded at the bathroom door. Linc pulled it open to find Jeff leaning against the open door frame. His second in command looked dapper in a dark suit. His left arm was caught up in a matching sling.

"You take care of it?" Linc asked.

"Yeah," said Jeff. "I did what you asked. I still don't think it's a good idea."

"But you did it?"

"Yes, I did it," Jeff said as he backed away to allow Linc to pass. "You're really going through with this?"

"Of course," said Linc.

Linc knew Jeff wasn't referring to the wedding. Linc was itching to get out of the cabin and walked down the aisle. There was just one thing he had to do first. A critical task he had to accomplish before his mission was complete.

"What if the other girls don't get married and they wind up losing this place?" Jeff asked.

"I can't help that."

That was tough for Linc to admit. He didn't want to fail that broader mission. Just the week he'd spent on this ranch had given him a renewed purpose in life.

He loved working with the horses each day. He loved caring for the land. What he loved most was the woman who walked by his side each day, the woman with who he'd spend the rest of his life with, looking in Scout's crystal blue eyes and finding clarity and peace.

"If we lost the ranch," he said, "then we'll rebuild someplace new. In the meantime, we work the objective. Have you made any headway with your mission with your Silver sister?"

Jeff looked away. It didn't look like he'd answer. Finally, he opened his mouth... and a knock sounded at the front door.

"That'll be for you," Jeff said as he slipped past to go to the door. Jeff opened the door to an empty space.

"Is he in there?" came Linc's soon-to-be-wife's voice.

"Yeah," grinned Jeff.

"Well? What's so important that it couldn't wait until he sees me at the end of the aisle in twenty minutes?"

"You'll have to ask him yourself." Jeff stepped outside and marched away.

Scout didn't come into view. "Linc? What's going on?"

"I need you to come in here," he said.

"You can't see me before the wedding. It's bad luck."

"Do you really believe that there is any chance I'm not putting a ring on your finger today and spending the rest of my life with you?"

A pause. And then a vision of white stepped into the door frame. All rational thought left Linc's brain at the site of Scout.

She was a vision in a simple white sundress. White cowboy boots hugged her shapely calves. A bouquet of colorful flowers was held in her hands.

Linc stepped toward her. His arms ached to pull her close. His lips were itching to have a taste of her. But Scout wasn't stepping into his arms. She stepped around him.

"Linc..." she breathed. That was all she managed.

She stopped in the center of the room and stared, her jaw slack. Linc watched her expression as her eyes roved the expanse of the mission wall. He'd removed all the sticky notes from the cabin, except the new mission he'd posted to this wall.

Linc came to stand behind Scout. For a moment, he worried he'd gone too far. But the tears pricking at the corners of her eyes told him he'd gone just the right amount.

On the wall was a collage of sticky notes. He'd gone for pinks and purples because he supposed those were girly. Though his Scout was far from a girly girl. Still, he'd wanted it to be pretty. And those pastel colors were pretty as they formed the shape of a heart.

Scout stepped up to the wall. Her right hand shook as she raised it. With trembling fingers, she pulled at the center sticky note. On the piece of paper was written a single statement.

Be the best husband to my wife.

"This is my new mission," said Linc. "I have a number of objectives and tasks."

Scout replaced the mission statement. Her fingers were no longer shaking. She laid her flat palm over the square patch of paper and pressed it back into the wall.

Her attention turned to the next post-it. On varying shades of purple slips of paper were the first of Linc's objectives.

Be a helpmate. Be a good father. Show my love.

"I don't have all the tasks written out yet," he said. "There are some blanks that need to be filled in."

"I can help with that," she said. Scout reached to the side table where Linc had left his materials. She picked up a blank note, a light green color, and wrote. Once she was done, she turned back to the wall and pressed the note amongst the others.

Beneath the objective *Show my love,* Scout posted a note that read *Task: kiss your wife every day —a lot.*

Scout set the pad down. She recapped the pen and placed it beside the post-its. Then she straightened in her white dress, looking anything but innocent.

"Well, soldier? You have your orders. Are you up to the task?"

"Yes, ma'am," Linc grinned. "I think I'm up for that task."

Linc pulled his woman, his world, into his arms. His kiss wasn't an assault. There was no need for it to be. He'd laid down any arms he might've held the moment he saw this woman. She'd conquered him, body and soul.

"How'd I do?" he asked when he broke the kiss.

"You're going to get a very good performance report, soldier."

"I love you." Linc pressed his forehead to hers. "I may have forgotten to tell you that before. But I want you to know it's true now and will be true every day of our lives together."

"It's okay. I'll remind you." Scout lifted her head to gaze up at him. "I love you, too."

Linc kissed her again. Not only his heart but his mind felt in tune with her. This was a process he would not need prompts to remember.

When he broke this last kiss, he turned to look at the mass of sticky notes he'd compiled to please this woman. "I think it'll take me a lifetime to complete these loving tasks, but I'm up for it."

"Me, too."

"Then we should probably get started on the first task," he said. "The one where we get married."

Linc held out his hand. Scout placed her hand in his. Together they walked out of the cabin and toward the aisle. In the distance, the horses whinnied their approval.

*J*eff kept his eye trained on the cabin in the distance. The door still hadn't opened. Either Linc had failed in his clerically romantic notion, and they were taking the office stationery down off the walls. Or he had won Scout over with his post-it notes of love, and they were even now anticipating their vows. In either case, Jeff didn't mind the wait. Not when the view was so lovely.

Saylor Silver had her hair down around her shoulders. The lush strands fell like waves around her face. Jeff envied each tendril that had the right to kiss her flushed cheeks.

Jeff was able to look his fill at the second eldest Silver sister. Her attention was diverted elsewhere.

Mostly her gaze was trained on the bouquet of colorful flowers in her hands. But every once in a while, she'd lift her head and look over at the bride's side of the aisle where guests were seated. Her blue eyes settled on one guest in particular.

A man sat with his arm drooped around the back of a pretty brown-skinned woman's chair. Brig had pointed the man out to Jeff earlier. The youngest Silver hadn't told Jeff the man's name, only his title. With a sneering lift to her lip, Brig had raised two fingers, as though in a curse, and labeled the man as The Boyfriend.

Jeff didn't need to ask whose boyfriend. Only one of the Silver sisters present was in a long term relationship. Though by looking at The Boyfriend's body language as he flirted with the woman seated next to him, it wasn't clear the man understood the term relationship or boyfriend.

The Boyfriend leaned in to whisper into his companion's ear. As the woman threw her head back and laughed, The Boyfriend blatantly looked down her top. Then he had the indecency to lick his lips.

Saylor fidgeted as the scene continued to play out under her nose. Under everyone's nose. Because they weren't the only ones looking at the two with open disdain. Some of those glances of the guests assembled traveled back to Saylor, which is when she would always drop her gaze to the ground.

Just as Jeff's mother always did.

Saylor had the same downcast eyes, as though she wasn't seeing the reality of her world, then it wasn't happening. She had the same helpless pinch to her lips, as though she were searching for the right words to make the man she loved only whisper sweet nothings for her ears alone. Her feet did the same restless tapping, as though she wanted to march over to The Boyfriend but knew it might end in her humiliation.

So she stayed still. She stayed quiet. She kept her gaze cast down.

Jeff felt a tingling in his palm. He wanted to ball his fingers into a fist and strike The Boyfriend. But it was his left hand that felt the tingle. The hand that had gone numb since he'd been caught in an explosion.

The doctors told him that from time to time, he might feel something there. The limb was numb, but it wasn't dead. This past week, Jeff had been feeling more and more sensations.

Like when he'd had his first glance of Saylor as she climbed out of the truck. Like when she'd passed him the salad at dinner, and her shoulder had brushed against his left side. Like when she'd bandaged him up in the barn, and her fingers had done quick, competent work of his injury.

His need to reach out to her, to offer her comfort. was overwhelming the thriving parts of him. So it was no wonder the sensation was seeping into his numb extremities.

"There they are," said Saylor. Her gaze was lifted to the cabin in the distance where Linc and Scout were making their way toward the outdoor ceremony. "You ready?"

Saylor slipped her hand through the crook of his left elbow. His left arm was done up in a sling that matched his suit so that it would look like he was leading her down the aisle like the others. When her fingers tucked into his side, Jeff felt an explosion of sensation at his ribs. The heat flooded his body, pooling in his heart and going up to his head.

The only thing he could think of was how to get her away from a man who clearly didn't know how to love this treasure in his keep. But was Jeff even qualified for the job?

His physical injury aside, there was still the case of his mental ones. This wasn't the first time he'd stood by in the face of such abuse. Could a man who witnessed his father hurt his mother emotionally, mentally, and physically every day of his young life truly be able to cherish a woman of his own?

It was a mission Jeff had to gather the courage to undertake. He'd made a pledge to the General. So, he was duty-bound to try.

*But the question isn't will Jeff do everything in his heart
to cherish Saylor,
it's can Saylor find the strength and confidence in herself
to believe she is worthy of such true and unconditional
love?
Find out in "His Pledge to Cherish"
Book 2 in the Silver Star Ranch romances.*

Grab Your Copy Now!

Shanae Johnson was raised by Saturday Morning cartoons and After School Specials. She still doesn't understand why there isn't a life lesson that ties the issues of the day together just before bedtime. While she's still waiting for the meaning of it all, she writes stories to try and figure it all out. Her books are wholesome and sweet, but her are heroes are hot and heroines are full of sass!

And by the way, the E elongates the A. So it's pronounced Shan-aaaaaaaa. Perfect for a hero to call out across the moors, or up to a balcony, or to blare outside her window on a boombox. If you hear him calling her name, please send him her way!

You can sign up for Shanae's Reader Group and receive a FREE NOVELLA in this world at

http://bit.ly/ShanaeJohnsonReaders

Also By Shanae Johnson

The Silver Star Ranch Romances

His Pledge to Honor

His Pledge to Cherish

His Pledge to Protect

His Pledge to Obey

His Pledge to Have

His Pledge to Hold

The Rangers of Purple Heart

The Rancher takes his Convenient Bride

The Rancher takes his Best Friend's Sister

The Rancher takes his Runaway Bride

The Rancher takes his Star Crossed Love

The Rancher takes his Love at First Sight

The Rancher takes his Last Chance at Love

The Brides of Purple Heart

On His Bended Knee

Hand Over His Heart

Offering His Arm

His Permanent Scar

Having His Back

In Over His Head

Always On His Mind

Every Step He Takes

In His Good Hands

Light Up His Life

Strength to Stand

The Rebel Royals series

The King and the Kindergarten Teacher

The Prince and the Pie Maker

The Duke and the DJ

The Marquis and the Magician's Assistant

The Princess and the Principal

www.ingramcontent.com/pod-product-compliance
Lightning Source LLC
Chambersburg PA
CBHW071804190726
48292CB00008B/2702